Two Ships

Illustrated
Tales From an Alternate
Steampunk History
Book 2

2nd Edition

Timothy M Dooley

Two Ships is actually two stories from different periods in the Alternate Steampunk History Series that collide with each other as the result of being caught up in time storms. One is the tale of the Minerva airship's one and only voyage under the command of Captain Cobb. The other is the first story from the adventures of Captain Lionheart and the maiden voyage of his starship the Onyx Tower.

As the tale of Two Ships takes you to different places and years, remember you're traveling through an illustrated alternate history. All of the books in this series are dedicated to all who enjoy science fiction and especially to those who remember Jules Verne and are into Steampunk.

Throughout this series, some of the characters are based on remarkable people in real life. The characters of Captain Lionheart and Margret Dana were directly inspired by Aerospace Engineering Directors; Peter M Leonhardt and Marjie Mattingly. In my thirty-five plus years' experience of working in the aerospace industry, both of them are clearly the most gifted individuals I have ever encountered and had the pleasure of working with.

Sincerely-

Timothy M Dooley

In the fabric of history, it is not uncommon to find woven patterns that were caused by unusual events that happened in spite of being highly unlikely or even considered impossible, yet they happened just the same. In the order of things, the one constant is the fact that sometimes the paths of unrelated events can and will cross each other; sometimes for better, sometimes for worse, sometimes for an age of enlightenment, sometimes for an age of darkness. But whatever the outcome, it is often the character of those involved who decide how the course of history will unfold from that time. In some instances, it's almost as though some of those involved already knew what to expect and what the eventual outcome will be. Throughout the centuries, there have been amazingly accurate predictions and prophecies of events to come. But how does anyone know the details of future events? Was it divine inspiration or was it something else?

1627, The Valley of Bones, Western Siberia

Under the light of a full moon, Krnobov stood alone on a small rocky crag that overlooked the valley. As he surveyed the sight before him, he began to feel a sense of accomplishment. "I think my time here has been one of the more enjoyable chapters of my life." he thought to himself. Just an hour earlier his Guardian had appeared before him saying that his time there would soon be coming to an end. For his own safety, he would have to move on. The Guardian always appeared as a shadowy apparition of a man who first came to him when he was very young, back in China. Since the Guardian first appeared, Krnobov felt his life had been given a purpose, a godly purpose to prune back humanity to prevent it from destroying itself. The Guardian always advised him on what path to take throughout his life and was never wrong. Now the time had come to leave Western Siberia. As he turned to leave, Krnobov stopped and turned back to take one last look at all he had accomplished. The vast area all around was clearly visible under the light of a full moon. As he looked out, he saw neither land nor soil, but thousands upon thousands of human bones that covered the valley as far as the eye could see. They were the last remains of those who had been exposed to the harmful rays of uranium. At night their bones had a faint glow that gave them a somewhat ghostly appearance. As Krnobov departed he wondered if the dead would ever reveal the truth of what happened out here.

1. THE GUARDIAN was an angelic shadowy figure that first appeared in the early life of the one who called himself Krnobov. The Guardian could see into the future and gave careful advice on every step of life to come.

1548, Wolf Pan Arkansas

Sitting alone in the balloon basket, Bruster "Tex" Cobb looked out over the countryside of Wolf Pen, Arkansas. He wasn't worried about drifting off anywhere. The thousand-foot tether made sure of that. The year was 1548. America had been locked in a brutal civil war for the last two years. Like so many, Cobb hated the war and would be glad when it was over so he could resume his rich-kid, ne'er-do-well lifestyle, primarily drinking. At least high up in an observation balloon he could have a little drink without having to hide it.

Cobb was born in Waco, Texas in 1527 and was the only son of Travis Cobb, a wealthy local entrepreneur who founded the Cobb Rose Company in 1515. Over the years it had grown into a corporation that supplied desired plants, nursery supplies, fertilizer, and roses to every state in the south. The company also produced cosmetic and medicinal products based on rose oil. As Bruster grew up, he became somewhat hard for his parents to handle. He was a dark, tall handsome Texan with a smooth southern demeanor. By the time he was in his late teens he became known as "Rubber Neck". The title came from his friends who saw him get slapped and punched by women that he groped when he was drinking. Actually, one out of a hundred liked it. The rest would just do their best to loosen his teeth. When the Great American War broke out in 1546, Travis used his influence to get Bruster stationed in an observation balloon. He felt it increased the odds of his son surviving the war.

For two years, Cobb sat in his balloon and observed the distant action of troop movements, all of which he reported. For him the isolation of his post was ideal. It made it a lot easier to have a little drink. The main thing he worried about was stumbling away from the basket after his balloon was pulled back down. At sunset it started to get cold. Bruster had been up for seven hours already. Unknown to anyone, he had a bottle and continued to have a drink to pass the time.

2. IN HIS USUAL UNIQUE MANOR, Bruster Cobb stood watch at his post in his observation balloon.

On the night of September 5th, it looked like it was going to be another dark boring night. Cobb heard the crack of gunfire off in the distance, then another. Moments later his detachment below began shooting back. Seeing the fire from the enemy's guns, he couldn't tell how many there were but could estimate their location. He quickly wrote down the information, placed it in a small pouch and threw it overboard. As the fighting continued, Cobb did his best to see what was happening below. He still couldn't determine the enemy's numbers. At least the moonless night made his presence less visible. After a short time, the fighting became more intense.

Cobb took another drink. As he did so, a stray bullet shot the bottle out of his hand. He became very angry. At the risk of alerting the enemy to his presence and becoming an easy target, he fired a flare rocket over what he thought the enemy's position might be. The flare overshot his intended area, but as it got closer to the ground, Cobb could see larger enemy reinforcements moving in from behind. His troops below started retreating. Fearing the enemy, they cut his tether as they departed. The balloon suddenly lunged upward, and Cobb was thrown against the basket floor. He realized there was a slight breeze blowing him directly toward the enemy's position. They were advancing slowly, but before reaching his troops Cobb could see there was a thick line of trees, they had to get through first. That gave him an idea. He began to release gas from the balloon. He started to come down slow at first then faster. He was headed directly for the thick tree line. The shooting became more intense. Cobb grabbed a single flare rocket, climbed out and hung on the far side of the basket, hoping it might help shield him from the gunfire below. Moments later his basket hit the treetops. Cobb did his best to hang on as long as he could, but was eventually tossed away from the basket, hitting several tree branches as he fell.

Cobb was back on the ground and bruised up all over. For the first time, he was glad he had been drinking. His body didn't hurt as much. He stumbled as fast as he could toward the direction of his troops. He knew the enemy would be upon the balloon any moment. When he was a short distance away, he turned and fired his flare rocket at the balloon, igniting it's hydrogen in a violent explosion. All of the surrounding trees were engulfed in fire. He could hear some of the enemy troops screaming as they were burned alive. Cobb continued to stumble. Suddenly, a shot hit his leg and he fell forward on his face. He tried to make a bandage from tearing off part of his shirt, but he was becoming dizzy and didn't have the strength to tear off as much cloth as he needed. Fearing he might be killed or become a prisoner of war, Cobb started to crawl as best as he could, but the pain was overwhelming and getting worse. After only a short distance he turned, looked back at his blood trail and became even dizzier and eventually passed out.

Cobb woke up to find himself on a cot in an army hospital. He was relieved to see he was back with his people. As he looked around, he could see an army nurse attending to someone nearby. Still dazed and confused, he tried to sit up, only to fall back from dizziness. "Where am I? How long was I out?" he asked.

"You're in an army hospital just south of Wolf Pen. You've been out for the better part of a day." She answered quietly as she came over. "Excuse me, General Esseks asked to be informed as soon as you were awake" she said as she started to leave.

"Wait, what happened? The last thing I remember, the union was advancing on our position. I was trying to get back to my detachment when I was shot."

"They were advancing, and had it not been for you setting off that fire, we would have been over run. The fire you set held them back long enough for reinforcements to arrive. It would seem you are a war hero Mr. Cobb, and the General wants to thank you personally." She answered as she turned and walked away.

Cobb was later credited for turning the tide of The Battle of Wolf Pen (as it later came to be known) from a loss to a standoff. Later that day Cobb was awarded a medal for bravery in the face of the enemy. His commanding officer, First Lieutenant Dorner, was quietly disgusted by the event. He was planning a court martial to charge Cobb for drinking on duty. Two days later Cobb was discharged from the hospital. His leg had improved, and he was walking with a cane. He was granted a three week leave and it was likely that an honorable discharge would follow.

3. **FROM A SHORT DISTANCE AWAY,** Cobb turned and fired his flare rocket at the balloon, igniting its hydrogen in a violent explosion. He was shot in the leg as he tried to get away.

His commanding officer, First Lieutenant Dorner came to visit Cobb before he left the hospital.

"Well Cobb, you may have been shot, but yet you managed to dodge another bullet," Dorner said.

"I've been meaning to talk to you about that sir. My recent experience has given me a different outlook. When my leave is up, I want to return to active-duty Sir."

"In God's name why would a rich pampered southerner with a drinking problem want to help fight in a war that we are likely to lose? Go home to your father's mansion son. I admit, after what you did back there proves you have your good points, but this this is no place for you," Dorner insisted as he started to walk away.

"Sir, after my leave I want to come back and resume my duty."

"It's out of the question son."

"Sir, my father has influence with the Texas senate. If necessary, I'll pull every string I can," Cobb said.

"I don't understand you Cobb. Up until you got shot, you couldn't wait to get out. It was my understanding your father arranged for you to be in the Balloon Corps to keep you out of the fighting. During your enlistment you have been in the brig three times for groping women while intoxicated. You know if you keep that up, one of these days that rubber neck of yours is going to snap off," Dorner said.

"It almost did...twice, Sir. I can't explain what happened back there. When I saw my detachment come under fire the whole war suddenly seemed real to me. If we lose this war, we will no longer have self-rule. Will be subject to Washington and leaders we don't like and didn't vote for. No, I want to see this thing through. If we lose our sovereignty, I can rest better knowing I did everything I could to stop it," Cobb said.

"I can respect that, but so help me Cobb if you go back to your drinking, groping lifestyle, I'll see to it that you get transferred to hell and not even your father can save you," Dorner warned.

Cobb returned to Waco and was surprised to see how everything looked dilapidated. Most of the businesses were closed, and many downtown buildings were deserted. The streets were in a state of disrepair. When he returned to the family estate, one of the conservatories had been converted into a makeshift hospital. Cobb was deeply moved by the sight of so many wounded. He later returned to the army and served out his tour of duty until the war ended two years later in 1550.

He didn't realize how much he enjoyed flying until after the war. On a subconscious level, he began to think of ways that would allow him to continue to fly. His father, Travis Cobb, expected his son to take an active role in his business along with his younger sister Billy Sue, but she had no interest in working for the company. She did, however, enjoy the lifestyle it provided. Bruster turned out to be a shrewd businessman. To him, business was like a high stakes card game. He enjoyed taking risks but in spite of the appearance of uncertainty, Bruster actually thought things through very carefully. It was clear to his father that the war had awakened something inside of him. Having helped restore his family business back to pre-war levels, Bruster began to think about flying again. Over time he persuaded his father to have a company balloon for advertising and flew it whenever he could. In spite of his father's early objections, the balloon turned out to be a hit at local state fairs. For a small fee, visitors could look out over Texas from a tethered balloon five hundred feet up.

1830, Lake Elizabeth, Arizona

Lionheart stood alone on his balcony as he looked out over the dark water of the man-made lake that surrounded his castle. It wasn't long after sunset that the stars began to appear in the sky above. As he looked up at the them, he felt he was close to discovering a key that could unlock the universe. Then he thought about all the events of his life that led up to this point.

Peter Edward Lionheart was born in Stratford, England in 1808. The maritime shipping empire founded by his great grandfather, Sir Erin Lionheart, made the family one of the most prominent in Europe. Peter was a gifted child. At the age of 12, he was the youngest to be admitted to Cambridge and as predicted, he excelled in mathematics and science. Because of the age difference between him and the other students, Peter often felt isolated. He did, however, enjoy being surrounded by college girls. Peter had a very bright personality and female students found him sweet and charming. It wasn't long before he started hosting dorm parties. During these parties he often wore a kingly robe, had a turkey leg in one hand and a large beer stein in the other. Needless to say, he quickly developed a reputation. On campus he became known as "Little Henry". There was yet another side to Peter. He loved to explore. Whenever the opportunity presented itself, he would be off on some expedition to the far ends of England, and eventually parts of Europe. His father, Samuel Lionheart, permitted it, but there were times when he became concerned for his son's safety.

In 1823 at the age of 15, Lionheart started his graduate work. He took a keen interest in a map that showed the magnetic and gravitational fields of the universe that had been published a year earlier by Dr. Markus Maraday. He asked his father if he could be sent to western America to learn how to oversee the company's operations there. His father quickly agreed. Even though Samuel had groomed Peter to run the shipping empire he knew deep down Peter had only minimal interest because in college he had discovered his real passion, astronomy. From that time on Peter had a plan.

Lionheart was sent to his new home in southern California and in less than two years he was placed in charge. At the age of 21 he was now one of the wealthiest men in America. Under his leadership, profits from his division had tripled by 1829. Although he was not yet directly involved in the scientific community, Peter began providing grants to individuals to further their endeavors. As a result, he became well known in that community. He was very happy with his situation. As long as profits flowed back to England, he was free to run this branch of his father's empire as he saw fit. Almost from the time he had arrived in America, Peter began diverting some of the company's funds to build another castle on his own private manmade lake in Arizona. His father allowed it, considering the company profits were up in spite of the added expense. It was completed in 1830, seven years after he first arrived in America.

There, he would begin research that he hoped would unlock some of the secrets of the universe. For many years he had something deep inside and now it was coming out. To his surprise, Lionheart came to the realization that his destiny was slowly unfolding like a map. He wasn't sure where it was going, but he had the feeling its course had been carefully laid out before he was born. Even though his work was kept secret, rumors of his science experiments in the castle began to circulate. Soon after, his facility was referred to as the "Dark Castle".

In 1831 at the age of 83 Samuel Lionheart passed away. To everyone's surprise, Peter's cousin Jane Dietrich, would assume Samuel's position in the Lionheart shipping empire in Europe, and Peter would have full ownership of operations in America. It was exactly what Peter planned. He never wanted to run all of the empire as it would take him away from his research. After attending his father's funeral in England, Lionheart returned to America to pursue his interests. With the full revenue from the American business, he was now free to pursue his interests on an unprecedented scale.

4. LIONHERT'S INFAMOUS DARK CASTLE.

Years earlier, when Lionheart was examining Dr. Markus Maraday's map of the universe, Lionheart began to wonder if it might be possible to obtain interstellar travel by means of distorting space itself. The idea first occurred to him when he was diving off the California coast in 1824. The water was very clear on that sunny winter day. Only 10 feet under the surface he floated motionless over the underwater seascape below. The motion of the surf was moving him back and forth, and yet he had almost no sensation of movement. That was compounded by the sight of the fish swimming around him who also were completely unaffected by the rolling landscape below. Just below his area, he could see the sand and kelp being swept back and forth with the rolling surf. He later came to the conclusion, If the space you occupy moves with you, it might be possible to move anywhere in the universe without the effects associated with movement. He later considered the reason why the movement of some stars and galaxies in the universe could not be explained by means of gravitational forces was because the space around them may actually be moving as well.

Lionheart believed if space could be expanded it would be a simple matter for a vehicle to move by riding just outside of the event bubble. The key to everything was a theoretical bomb that he referred to as a singularity device, which could contract space by means of the Dark Energy it created. In 1833 Lionheart began conducting space altering experiments at his facility in Arizona. In order to see the result of altering space, he created an ionized gas sphere in a vacuum. As the space was altered, he could visually observe the effect.

As his early experiments progressed, one possible conclusion Lionheart held turned out to be true. As the existence of the temporary Dark Energy (produced by the singularity devise) comes to an end, so does its influence on the surrounding space. The expanded space bubble inside the sphere of ionized gas would begin to contract back to normal. He also observed that there appeared to be no effect on the ionized gas inside the space distortion area. After the space expansion experiment, he concluded a ship on the event horizon would move out as space expanded but it would move back to its initial position when space returned to its original state.

5. **WHILE HE FLOATED IN THE ROLLING SURF,** Lionheart came to the conclusion the rolling of space itself may also be possible, and if so, it might be possible to move anywhere in the universe without the effects of moving.

6. AT THE DARK CASTLE, Lionheart begins his experiments in distorting space itself.

After several sleepless nights, Lionheart came up with the idea that in order for an object, (or ship) to move from point A to point B by means of space distortion, two artificial events would be needed. One would expand space while the other would contract space. A moving wave effect would be created in the event horizon between the two. This effect would move both distortions in a single liner direction. To do this a second singularity device would be needed. This one would contract space around it by giving a false impression of being a black hole. Unlike the black hole, its effect would also be temporary and less severe.

The next step would be to create a spacecraft that could deploy both expanding and collapsing devices to see if a space wave could actually be created. It would be a long time to get the results of such an experiment. To test the ship properly, it would have to be deployed beyond the solar system prior to distorting space and even with the fastest rockets it would take years to get the ship into position.

When the hard reality of just setting up his initial experiment was most likely years away, Lionheart took a step back. Consumed in deep thought, he went out on the balcony and gazed at the dark waters of the lake surrounding his castle. It was now 1835, two years since his experiments in space distortion began. He wondered if there were others who might be pursuing the same goal.

A month later, Lionheart received word that a contemporary physicist in California was working to develop an internal drive engine and was seeking further funding. Lionheart knew if such an engine could be developed, the years it would take to get his spacecraft into position could be accomplished in a matter of days. Upon hearing the news, he became ecstatic. Lionheart arranged to fly to California the next day.

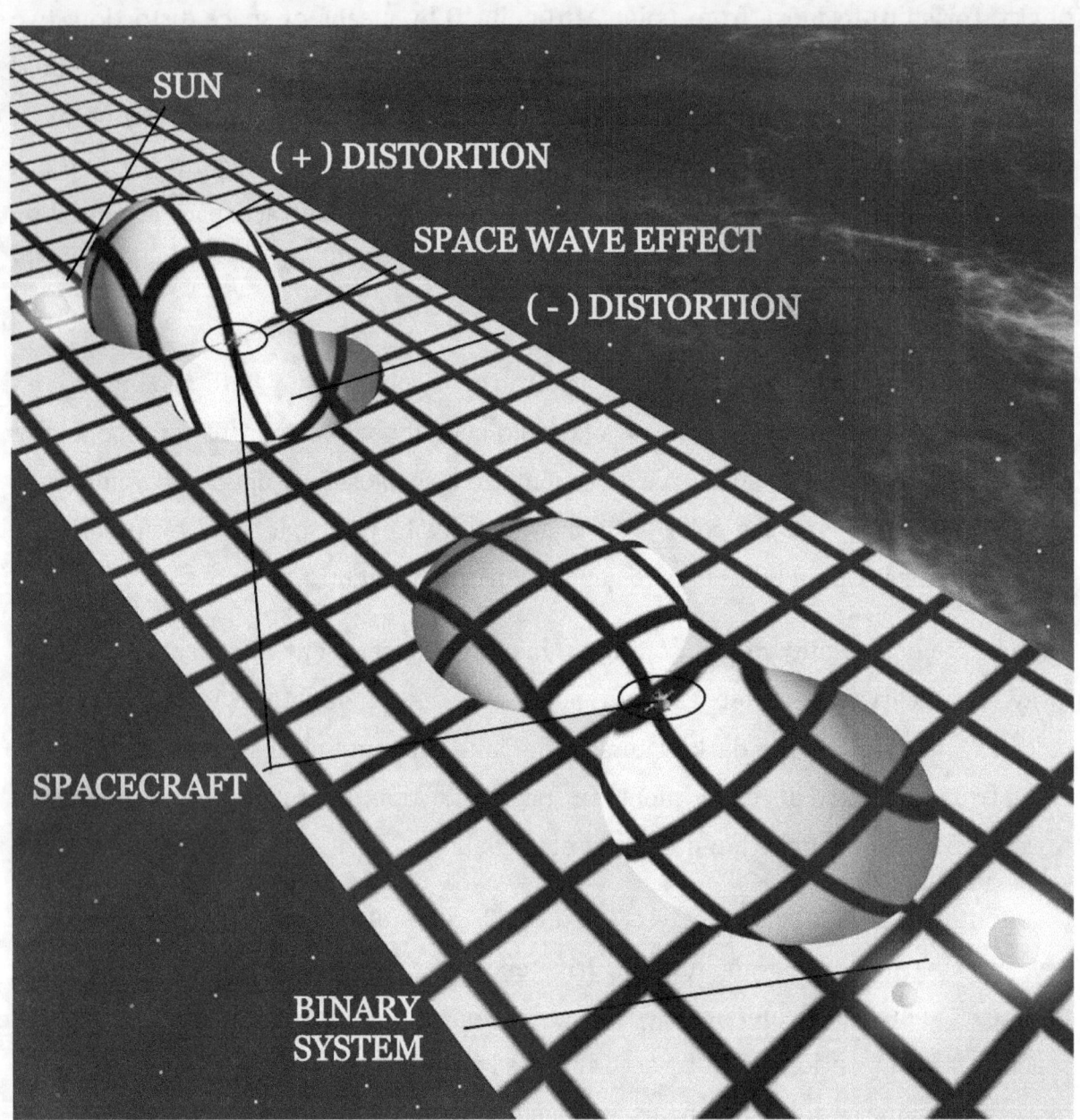

7. LIONHEART'S SPACE DISTORTION- Positive and negative distortion creates a space wave at the departure point from the sun. Space distortion returns to normal near the intended destination, in this case a binary system.

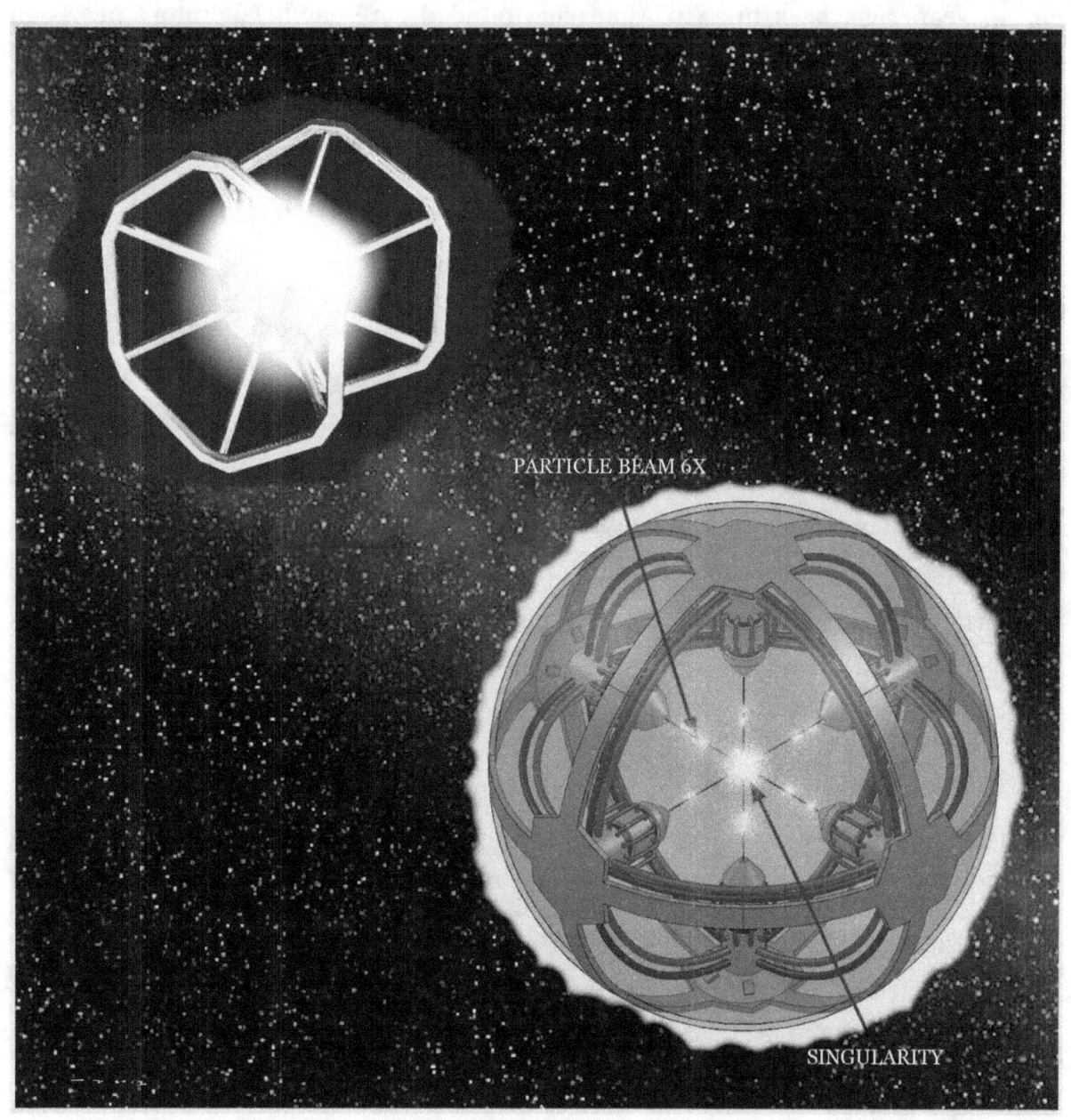

PARTICLE BEAM 6X

SINGULARITY

8. **LIONHEART'S SINGULARITY DEVISE** was basically a sphere that contained three pairs of particle beam guns. The pairs were positioned in the X, Y and Z axis. When fired at the point at the sphere's center a temporary singularity would form that could either expand or contract surrounding space for a short time.

The contemporary physicist was Margret Dana. Lionheart recalled first hearing of her 16 years ago, back in 1819 when she founded a research laboratory near San Antonio Lake. Since that time there had been quiet stories floating around the scientific community that Dana had been conducting experiments that involved the exchange of normal matter for matter of greater mass (dark matter) from another part of the universe. Rumors of something called "The Portal Project" began to circulate after an accident occurred at Dana's laboratory in 1831.

Lionheart and Dana became immediate friends and developed a close liaison that lasted many years. Lionheart not only helped fund her research, but also had a great interest in it and helped wherever he could. Beyond their work, they often played mental chess. She was one of the few people that rivaled his intellect. After their first meeting, Lionheart realized that he wasn't the only one who had been inspired by the work of Markus Maraday's map of the known universe that was first published back in the early 1820's. Maraday's map gave detailed information on the gravitational and magnetic fields. Unlike Lionheart, Dana's interest was along different lines.

Before discussing the internal drive engine's current project development, Dana revealed a history of its development and how the initial discovery happened quite by accident. She opened by saying the rumors and stories he might have heard of the portal project were only false, exaggerated tales of dark research. The actual portal project wasn't originally intended to exchange matter for dark matter. The original intent was to create a gateway portal that would allow the exchange of matter for matter from a distant part of the universe for observation only.

The fact that Dana's portal project had successfully teleported a person from California to England in 1827 was kept secret. It was known only to a very few and her backer, Dr. Serco. He was the only one who was still around. The others had been teleported to the paradise of their choice. By this time Dana and Serco were the only live people at the facility. The entire staff was mechanical personnel.

9. **ABOVE: THE DANA REASURCH LABORATORY** near San Antonio Lake, California.

Dana told Lionheart her interest in the possibility of exchanging matter began in 1819 when her observation of atoms revealed they appear to phase in and out of existence. Dana concluded when atoms disappear, they do not cease to exist they simply exist in another part of the universe or a parallel universe for a brief time. She wondered if it would be possible to create an environment where atoms from another part of the universe could be exchanged for their local counterpart she was observing. If the control factor wasn't based on equal mass, normal matter could be briefly exchanged for matter of a different mass. At the time, Dana's goal was to study the properties matter that affected parts of the observable universe she was interested in.

Like the universe, Maraday's map of its gravitational and magnetic fields was constantly changing. Dana had developed a way to open a gateway almost anywhere but was unable to calculate the exact place to capture matter she was interested in observing. Too little mass would create a vacuum effect. Too much could have the same effect as a black hole. At best her observations and calculations could only be approximate.

Dana's initial attempt at matter exchange consisted of what she called an "In-Line Particle Accelerator". It consisted of a long tubular vacuum chamber that was divided into thirds. At one end, a small energy gun fires charged particles into the first chamber. As the particles reach the end of the first chamber, they enter a portal where they are exchanged for matter from another part of the cosmos. Moving at the same speed and direction as the initial matter, the heaver matter continues to the far end of the second chamber where it passes through a second portal and is exchanged back for normal matter. The normal matter continues on through the third chamber until it strikes an inertia plate at the far end of the chamber. The system works much like a bullet fired at a target range except for a brief length of travel (long before striking the target) the bullet is from another part of the universe.

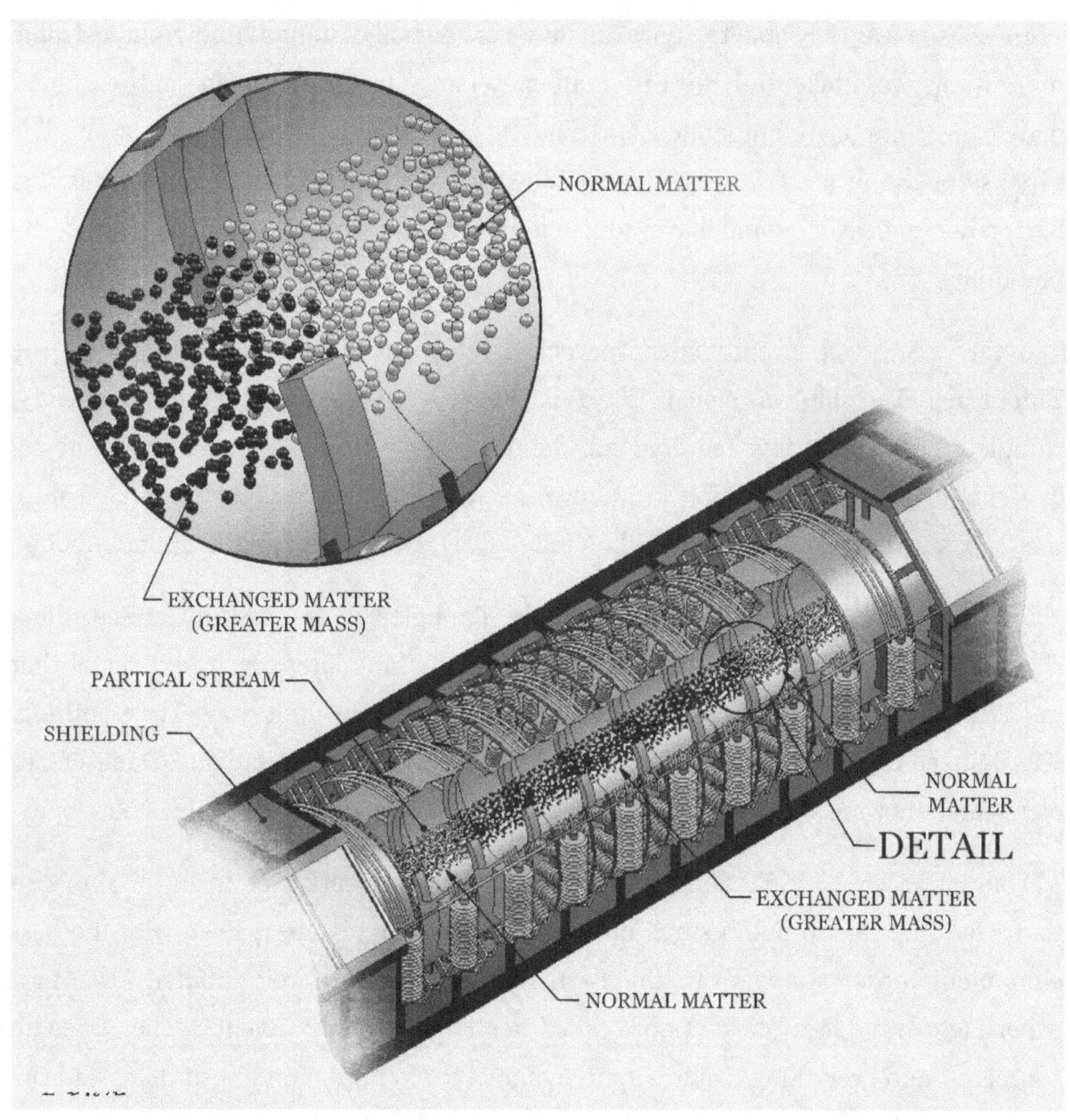

NORMAL MATTER

EXCHANGED MATTER
(GREATER MASS)

PARTICAL STREAM

SHIELDING

NORMAL
MATTER

DETAIL

EXCHANGED MATTER
(GREATER MASS)

NORMAL MATTER

10. THE SECOND CHAMBER of Dana's in-line particle accelerator was where normal matter was exchanged for matter of greater mass. Even though the flow of particles was actually a short burst that only lasted less than a micro-second, it was long enough for Dana to measure the heaver mass and make a better determination for locating a safe place in the universe to pull heaver matter from.

Since Dana was only able to approximate where to pull distant matter from, extreme precautions were taken for the first matter exchange experiment. The entire system had to be completely automated and had to take place at a remote location. The expense of the project was enormous. Had it not been for Dana's main backer, Dr. Serco, her endeavor would have concluded with only a thesis that suggested the possibility.

In early 1830 a lone automated spacecraft set down on a distant asteroid in the Kuiper belt. The ship was called "The Triangle". It contained a miniature laboratory, complete with everything required for Dana to carry out her first matter exchange experiment. The Triangle ship's location was so distant that a second automated ship, the "Nexis", (that was only a few million miles away) was sent to give it commands.

Back on Earth, after receiving word that the Triangle had successfully landed, Dana signaled the Nexis to proceed with the experiment. Dana later received a signal that the Triangle's energy gun had fired getting the experiment underway. Then nothing. She signaled the Nexis to proceed to the Triangle's location to investigate. Dana's team of researchers were stunned by the images sent back from Nexis long range telescope.

Dana knew it wasn't possible to determine the exact location point in the universe that would be safe to pull a small micro sample of heavy matter. Even with the best equipment, observations from the Earth and Moon were very limited. The first experiment produced what Dana called a "High Gravity Event". The Triangle spacecraft and everything inside a sphere diameter of approximately 50 miles had the appearance of being pulled into a miniature black hole. Gravitational measurements of the area made after the experiment revealed nothing unusual. It suggested the heavy matter had been exchanged back for normal matter. Dana wondered how that would be possible if the Triangle spacecraft had also been consumed by the event.

11. THE TRIANGLE SPACECRAFT'S LAST LOCATION was marked by a 50-mile-wide bowl feature on the asteroid where it landed. Even though Dana's team was somewhat horrified by the site, Dana wasn't. She knew of the possibility. That is why she had the first experiment done in a remote location.

Despite the outcome of the first experiment, the measurement of mass and the location it was pulled from allowed Dana to much more accurately pinpoint a safer place to pull matter from. Before any construction for the matter exchange experiments started, Dana had already reasoned a minimum of three labs would be needed before the exact heavy mass density needed could the determined. She also reasoned that the first experiment would likely be the most dangerous.

The data from the first experiment allowed Dana to have two small test labs constructed on the far side of the Moon. There were many settlements on the Moon by this time and the building of new structures would not likely draw any attention. Despite the enormous expense, Dana's main backer, Dr. Serco, kept the money flowing in.

In 1831, almost a year to the day, the second matter exchange experiment took place. Like the first, the experiment was completely automated. Dana insisted no one be present. The second experiment produced another high gravity event as Dana expected, but because Dana was able to make more precise calculations, the event was far less severe.

12. MARGRET DANA 1831

13. **THE SECOND MATTER EXCHANGE EXPERMENT** went much better than the first, but it left the lab severely damaged. **ABOVE:** Working at the control station, Dana made final checks before the second matter exchange experiment. **BELOW:** Even though the heavy matter of the second experiment was far less massive than the first, the smaller effect left by the high gravity event" damaged the lab beyond repair.

14. **DANA REVEALES THE HISTORY** of her matter exchange experiments to Lionheart. After Dana told Lionheart of the third experiment's success, she felt Lionheart's arrival was timely. Dr. Serco's financial backing was becoming less and less in light of the enormous expense of the experiments. Lionheart was excited by her work and was only too happy to help finance whatever she needed to continue.

In concluding the history of her mater experiments with Lionheart, Dana revealed their meeting was most timely, not only because of his support but also because a new test chamber was just completed at her San Antonio Lake facility. Dana's initial interest in creating a cylindrical ring test chamber was to allow heavy matter to be observed continuously. In addition to its new configuration, another new ability was now the fields in the exchanger could be altered without the need for pre calibration. Although Dana had calculated the alternate mass intensity, the exchanger could now be adjusted on command. Both Dana and Lionheart were delighted by the result.

On the night of August 12, 1835, Dana and Lionheart made an incredible discovery. During the course of an experiment, the exchanger was accidentally adjusted above its intended limit. During that moment the chamber moved slightly away from its center axis toward the direction of the exchanged matter. Safeguards in the system shut everything down immediately. After reviewing her observations both Dana and Lionheart concluded the dark mass in the exchanger, being of greater mass than the ring particles, created a greater centrifugal outward force that became strong enough to move the entire chamber off its center. In the weeks that followed it became clear that she had discovered a practical means of using exchanged matter. She called her new discovery "Centrifugal Drive". The next step would be to construct a portable centrifugal chamber that could be controlled by adjusting the level of exchanged mass.

With the data collected, Lionheart suggested another chamber should be constructed but this one would be on a movable platform. Dana suggested a custom rail car. In 1838 the new portable ring chamber was completed on a custom rail flat car. In spite of the great lengths to miniaturize its components as much as possible, the "Centrifugal Drive Engine" as it was now called, was still simply too large and heavy to be supported by any known rail line. In addition to a custom flat car, a special four rail track that could withstand the weight of several trains was also built.

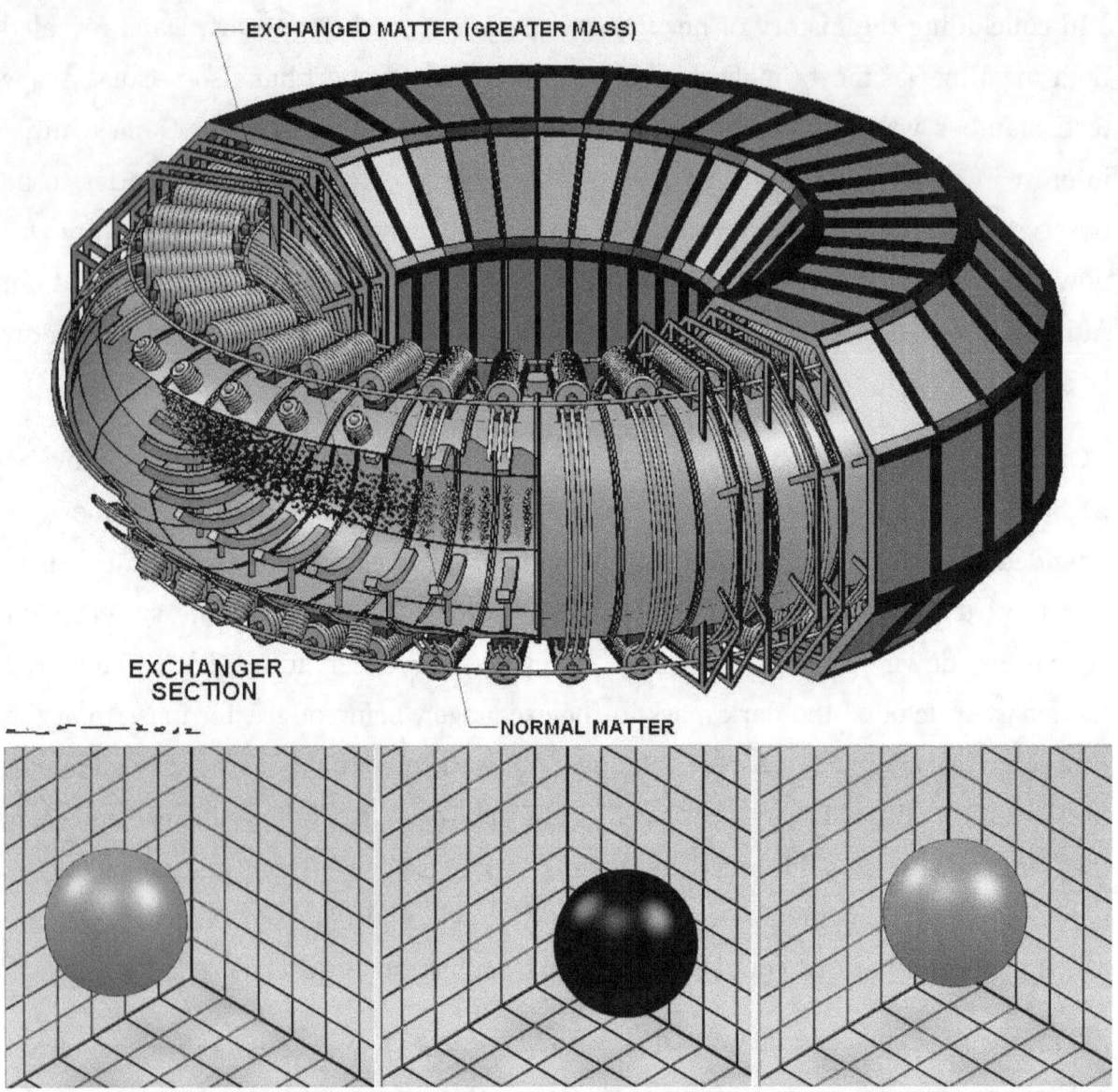

EXCHANGED MATTER (GREATER MASS)

EXCHANGER
SECTION

NORMAL MATTER

15. **DANA'S CYLINDRICAL RING TEST CHAMBER. Upper:** A partial cutaway view of ultra-low mass particles traveling in a circular chamber. As the particles pass through the Exchanger Section, they are traded for particles of a slightly heavier mass. They are then traded back again as they pass out of the Exchanger Section. **Lower Right and Left:** represent normal matter. **Lower Center:** Represents temporary Heavy Matter.

16. **THE FIRST PRACTICAL TEST** of the internal drive engine took place on a remote part of the Arizona desert, not far from Lionheart's Dark Castle. The magnets in the centrifugal chamber required enormous amounts of power to hold the particle stream in place. Early on it was decided only a uranium steam generator could provide that kind of power. The test was successful.

Among his other interests, Lionheart had a small fleet of ships at his disposal. He arranged for one of them (the Huron) to be pulled from service, partly dismantled, and rebuilt on his private lake. The Huron was rechristened the "Euphemus", and testing began almost straightaway. Powered with an internal drive engine, the Euphemus did not have a propeller. Even at reduced power the Euphemus wake splashed up 20 feet high on the Castle walls as it passed by. After six months of testing, the potential of the Centrifugal Drive Engine was clear.

17. LIONHEART WAS SO PLEASED WITH THE RESULT; he commissioned a painting of the Euphemus cruising on Lake Elizabeth.

It wasn't long after, during a quiet dinner, Lionheart revealed his plans to Dana to build the first experimental spacecraft that was based on Centrifugal Drive. At this time Lionheart insisted the new engine be simply referred to as the "Dana Engine". Although she had already thought of a flying application she was delighted and impressed by the detail of Lionhearts' plans. The craft looked like anything other than a spacecraft. It actually looked more like a refinement tower in a chemical factory.

The spacecraft consisted of three modules stacked on top of one another. It was later referred to as the mechanical snow man. The lower enclosure housed the uranium steam generator that would provide power. The mid enclosure was spherical and contained the centrifugal drive chamber. Above the centrifugal chamber was the four-member crew module. Because of the vehicles' excessive weight, it had eight legs. Basically, Lionheart's design was for a ship that could hover at high altitude like a balloon or once in space could maintain a constant one G pull toward a given destination. If it worked, travel time between the planets could be reduced from years to days.

Just inland from the Lake Elizabeth was a quiet secluded valley. There, Lionheart had an airship hanger that would be used for the new ship's construction. As work on the ship began there was constant effort to miniaturize components. As a result, the completed ship was two thirds the size of the original plans. The finished spacecraft was christened "The Zephyr".

In 1843 the Zephyr was ready for testing. During the next several months they had the craft hover a few feet above the ground. As testing progressed, Dana and Lionheart flew the craft from the airfield valley over to the castle and landed in its courtyard.

18. **THE ZEPHER HOVERS ONLY A FEW FEET** off the ground at Lionheart
Field, Arizona.

19. IN THE NEXT PHASE OF TESTING, Lionheart and Dana had the Zepher hover at the edge of space in a high-altitude test.

In 1844 they began conducting tests where the Zephyr was slowly flown to the edge of space and back almost exactly as it would have been using a high-altitude balloon. Testing the Zephyr outside the Earth's atmosphere began in 1845. Because of the ships' ability to maintain a constant force it would not be necessary to orbit the Earth to maintain altitude. Early on both Dana and Lionheart decided a spacecraft equipped with internal drive would work best in space because it would fly at a constant acceleration of one G, then, at mid journey began slowing at a rate of one G until reaching its destination. The Zephyr made its first Lunar landing in 1847. The one-way trip from Lionheart field took less than four hours. Dana and Lionheart determined the Zepher could reach Pluto's orbit in just under 18 days.

On its first flight to Mars there was a malfunction during the halfway turning maneuver that caused the craft to spin out of control like a twirling baton. For almost two hours crew members were pinned to the bridge ceiling and the power chamber floor. The Zepher had traveled four million miles off course by the time the spin was recovered. Despite the mishap, it still reached Mars in only four days. It was becoming clear the internal drive engine would open a frontier boom in the solar system, especially around the outer planets.

Even though off-world rocket travel had been around for more than a century, now, a means existed that could move mass payloads of people and materials to anywhere in the solar system in a short time. In 1850, to promote Dana Drive, Lionheart, Dana and two others flew the Zephyr on a grand solar system tour. The trip was highly successful.

20. **IN 1847 THE ZEPHER SPACECRAFT REACHED THE MOON** in only four hours.

21. **TO TEXT AND PROMOTE THE INTERNAL DRIVE ENGINE,** Dana,

Lionheart with two others flew the Zepher on a month long grand solar system tour in

1850. After returning to Earth, it was clear that the Dana Engine would revolutionize

space travel.

22. AFTER THE ZEPHER was flown on a solar system tour in 1850, Lionheart turned his attentions back to his space distortion experiments. With Dana's help, a new spacecraft similar to the Zephyr was constructed. The new ship was completed on June 10th, 1862, and was christened the Icarus.

Unlike the Zephyr spacecraft, the Icarus was actually an unmanned flying bomb. Its mission was to leave the solar system using its internal drive engine. Once outside the system it would release and detonate the singularity devices that Lionheart calculated would create a temporary distortion effect that would carry the ship exactly one light year away before the space around the ship returned to normal. At that point the ship would detonate a uranium bomb. Back on Earth, Lionheart would train his telescope on the precise location in the sky where the blast could be observed if all went well.

23. **OUT, BEYOND THE SOLAR SYSTEM** the Icarus fired its singularity devices in opposite directions.

24. **THE ICARCUS DEPARTED EARTH** on July 7th, 1863. At the Dark Castle observatory exactly one year, 23 days, and 57 minutes later Lionheart and Dana observed a bright uranium explosion exactly where it should be. It worked.

Almost at once Lionheart began construction of a new ship, the Elizabeth. Like the Icarus, it too was based on the Zephyr design, only its crew compartment was more like that of a space station, allowing for a long duration.

25. **THE STARSHIP ELIZABETH** was completed in late 1867.

26. ON APRIL 12TH 1868, Lionheart, and a crew of three others departed Earth for the Alpha Centauri system. Twenty-four days after Earth departure, the Elizabeth was as the edge of the solar system and the order was given to fire the singularity devices.

27. **THE VIEW FROM ALTERED SPACE** after the singularity devices fired.
Upper: As the forward space condensed, the stars ahead appeared to collapse into a
ball. **Lower:** As the space behind the ship expanded, the stars appeared to expand
outward forming a dark void.

As Lionheart expected, there was no sensation of movement. Approximately 23 hours later the stars all around the ship returned to normal, with the exception that formation of nearby stars was different. They were now less than three light years from their original position. Three suns appeared ahead. One was much closer than the others. It was Proxima Centauri. When space returned to normal, they were just outside its system and the three light year trip from our Sun had taken less than a day.

On May 6, 1869, the starship Elizabeth returned to Earth. To everyone's surprise, Lionheart and his crew were only a year older. Lionheart theorized because his ship was stationary in the ship's altered space and it was the space surrounding the ship that was moving, any possible outside effects of time and space did not apply. This meant a traveler inside an altered, contained space that was moving could journey to other star systems in real time. Lionheart made the most of his resources. In addition to visiting three nearby stars, he also mapped and charted twenty-three planets, thirty-one moons, twelve planetoids and two major asteroid rings. Among them, three planets and two moons were Earth like. With the exception of a water covered world, the Elizabeth starship landed on all the rocky planets. They all had life of some kind. The one moon where the ship didn't land was mostly covered by a dark ocean. Lionheart christened it 'Dark Neptune'. There, with its internal drive engaged, the Elizabeth hovered just a few feet above the water surface as Lionheart studied the area.

Based on the first venture to another star system, life turned out to be far more abundant in the universe than anyone had imagined. Lionheart studied many life forms very carefully but didn't bring back any samples for fear of contamination. When questioned about what he had seen he often answered, "God separated solar systems by light years for a reason". There were scratches on Elizabeth's hull, and they were not caused from the ship scraping against rocks. The voyage was a resounding success and Lionheart's name was etched in the book of history as one of its greatest explorers. Elizabeth's logbook was later known as Astro Voyage and became required reading at several deep space exploration academies. It also inspired scripts for several movies.

28. **WHILE HOVERING ABOVE THE WATERS** of Dark Neptune, the starship Elizabeth had an encounter with a large hungry sea creature.

There was one place Lionheart didn't tell anyone about. It was an Earth-like planet known as Proxima b. Its atmosphere wasn't breathable, but the temperature was similar to that of Earth along the terminator. Unlike the Earth, most of the land was rocky and barren. When Lionheart was there, he discovered a valley that was surrounded by unusual rock formations that reminded him of Arizona. He christened it "The Totem Valley". As far as they could tell it was the only place on the planet that had moss growing on the rocks everywhere.

Lionheart was overwhelmed with a sense of déjà vu in the Totem Valley. He decided to stay there for several days to see if he could find out why it triggered such strong feelings. On the last day Lionheart hiked out alone away from the ship to an area no one had yet explored. He wasn't expecting to find anything but what he found changed his life forever. He had discovered an obelisk made of stone. It was a crude stone likeness of a pyramid with a sphere in its top, it also had a worn encryption that he could barely read under the heavy moss growing out of it. It was in English and read simply "Lionheart".

He was stunned by the sight of it. For a moment the possibility of it being placed there by advanced aliens or supernatural beings crossed his mind. The sight of it triggered something in his mind. A cold chill came over him as if he had seen a ghost. Then he remembered drawing sketches of a similar object in his childhood. He remembered his mother asking him about his drawings and telling her they were of a magic powerful castle. Now, out here, light years away from Earth, there was an exact likeness of what had been on his mind. Lionheart told no one about his discovery in the Totem valley, not even his crew. Having seen the obelisk Lionheart felt he had a destiny. He had to build his castle. He began to realize his magic castle wasn't a castle at all, but rather a grand starship, one that had been in the back of his mind for over 60 years. He had to make his dream come to pass.

29. **LIGHT YEARS AWAY FROM EARTH,** in the Totem Valley on Proxima b,
Lionheart makes an incredible discovery.

1553, Waco Texas

In the three short years that followed the civil war, the Cobb Rose Company rose to levels no one thought possible. The balloon rides Bruster gave on the company estate revealed a huge market for tourism. By 1551 no visit to Texas was complete without seeing Cobb Rose Park. The idea of creating a grand park was inspired by Bruster from his memories of parks he visited in Europe. That same year construction began on a new project Bruster inspired. It would become known as the Cobb Rose Castle. The castle was mostly a grand arboretum and botanical garden that was the largest of its kind in the world. The Castle was completed in 1553.

With all the business success Bruster had been a part of, he never lost interest in flying. Shortly after the castle was completed, Bruster had an idea of constructing a balloon ship that could fly anywhere in the world. It was inspired by a balloon ship story in the paper written by Professor Robertson. Cobb's justification for presenting such an idea to his father was to be able to gather flower samples from distant lands to use for cross breeding experiments. It was a considerable expense. But considering the success Bruster had with balloon advertising, the grand park, the castle, and the fact that the company had tripled its business since he took an active role, his father agreed. For a project of this magnitude, the backing of the Cobb Rose Company would not be enough. They would need investors. At that time much of the world was still unexplored. It came as no surprise that John Malvern of Malvern Cosmetics and James Raleigh would take an interest. Raleigh was an associate who had many dealings with Travis Cobb over the years using rose oil for his cosmetic products. Raleigh's main interest was exploring the interior of South America. The jungles were rumored to have many unknown exotic plants. A condition of John Malvern's involvement was that his son, Robert Malvern, accompany the expedition. The Cobb's quickly agreed to the condition because Robert was a world-renowned botanist, and his expertise would be greatly appreciated.

30. **COBB ROSE CASTLE** was the largest arboretum and botanical garden in the world. It had thousands of visitors every year including dignitaries from all over the world.

As the pursuit for potential investors for the balloon ship project continued, Travis Cobb also received an inquiry from the Union Navy (the same navy his son fought against years earlier) that was totally unexpected. They expressed an interest in leasing the ship to explore an area off the southeast United States where many ships had vanished without a trace, a place known simply as "The Triangle". In the end, finding investors turned out to be easier than Travis Cobb first thought, so much so that he was surprised no one had pursued a balloon ship project before.

Having investors meant having outside influences on the design of the ship, most of which the Cobb's agreed too. But the one thing Bruster had trouble with was the addition of a large gas filled rooster on the top of the ship. Minerva Cobb (Bruster's mother) had a love for roosters. There were statues, plates, and even stained-glass windows in the kitchen, throughout Cobb Castle, and had it not been for Travis' intervention, Bruster would have been named Rooster. As a result of his mother's fetish, Bruster quietly hated roosters.

Another aspect of the project Bruster was uncomfortable with was having Dianna Raleigh, the daughter of James Raleigh, on board. Her presence had been a condition of James Raleigh's investment into the project. The last time Bruster saw Dianna was several years before the war and things didn't go well. He had been drinking, tried to grope her, and she broke his thumb. Bruster's father, on the other hand, liked the idea of having Dianna on board. Deep down, Travis Cobb respected her for giving his son a taste of his own medicine and liked James Raleigh's condition, but he kept it to himself. With her as second officer they would stand a better chance if they ran into something. Like Bruster, Dianna had also been a war hero. She grew up sailing with her father. During the civil war she had been given charge of a small cargo vessel with the mission of re-supplying soldiers on Galveston Island. During a fire fight she and her crew set fire to their ship just before ramming an enemy warship. To ensure hitting the target, she stayed on board to steer the ship until the last possible moment before jumping off the stern. Minutes later, the enemy ships magazine exploded, and both ships sank.

31. BRUSTER COBB QUIETLY HATED ROOSTERS.

Several years had passed since Cobb last saw Raleigh. Unlike him, she didn't come into her father's business after the war. She became a ship's captain running freight back and forth from South America. She had a reputation for being strong and fiercely independent. He wondered how clearly she would remember their last meeting. For a brief moment he even felt a little embarrassed about having been a drunken groper.

Cobb entered the study of his father's mansion. In it was a large table with several drawings of the new ship spread out all across it. As Cobb looked at the plans, he wondered if his first meeting with Raleigh would be awkward after all these years. He didn't have to wait long.

"Well, Bruster, It's been a long time, how's the thumb?" He turned around to see her smiling at the doorway behind him. Cobb was somewhat taken back by her looks and wondered why she never married.

"It still hurts a little when it rains," he responded with a faint smile. She came closer and he showed her the plans to the ship. He was surprised to see they got along better than he thought, as long as he treated her with respect.

A big part of the project, possibly more than the balloon ship, was building a facility large enough to house its construction. Several ideas were put forth, but in each case, there was one main problem, the weather. After a careful review of plans submitted, structural engineers concluded it was unlikely any building large enough to house a balloon ship would stand up to a moderate tornado. Unless a solution could be found, the ship hanger would have to be built in a state that had milder weather. The final solution came from a source no one expected; Sir Keven Butchart of the Butchart mining company. Butchart owned a depleted strip mine just southwest of Waco. Unlike most of his mines this one was particularly narrow and steep. In many respects it was more like a crater. Its opening was approximately 300 feet in diameter with a depth of 400 feet. Butchart had no prior association with Travis Cobb, but his wife however, Merlyn Butchart, was a different story. She was an avid botanist who created a beautiful world re-renowned garden in Canada that saw thousands of visitors every year. Her Garden was created from one of her husband's depleted strip mines. For years she associated with Minerva Cobb. She also helped in the planning of Cobb Rose Castle, but she expressed her concerns of the castle's ability to withstand tornadoes.

Sir Keven Butchart suggested the mine could be covered over with a removable roof that could withstand a Texas storm. The Cobbs were intrigued with the idea. Butchart suggested, before going any further, the Cobbs should study the feasibility of such a hanger. Several plans were later submitted to their structural engineers. After hearing the plan was feasible and cheaper than any alternative, Cobb sat down with Butchart to negotiate a price. Butchart said he would sell the mine on one condition, his son, Hermes Butchart be allowed to go on the balloon ships maiden voyage. Travis Cobb saw no immediate problem and agreed to the condition. The Cobb Rose Company purchased the property for $50,000, (a considerable sum at the time). Later, Bruster Cobb arranged to meet Hermes Butchart to see if there would be any personality problems and what kind of work he would be best suited for once on board. For Cobb, it was very important that the crew had compatible personalities. At the meeting, Cobb was surprised to see Hermes mother, Merlyn, attending. Shortly after the meeting started, the reason for her presence became all too clear. Hermes spoke only in broken sentences and seemed incoherent at times. He was autistic. Later, Cobb wondered if his father had been too hasty with Butchart's condition. He knew there would have to be another crewman who would keep watch on Hermes at all times.

After their meeting, Merlyn had a word in private with Bruster. She told Bruster even though her son was autistic he had the ability to see into the future. She showed Bruster several sketches Hermes did before their family heard of any balloon ship project. The Hermes sketches closely matched the actual plans of the balloon ship. Bruster was somewhat taken back by what he saw. There was also a sketch of what looked like a floating castle. Neither Merlyn nor Bruster knew what to make of it. There were other things Hermes told his mother about the balloon ship's maiden voyage, but Merlyn kept it to herself. Bruster knew having a seer on board could create problems among crew members who were superstitious. He knew Hermes would have to be watched only by someone he trusted, and if anyone asked, the story would be Hermes came on the voyage because he was a close family member.

32. **PREVIOUS DRAWINGS OF FUTURE EVENTS** created by Hermes Butchart are revealed to Bruster Cobb by Merlyn Butchart.

The hanger project became known as "Crater Hanger" and was completed in September 1554. The main problem was water had to be constantly pumped out. The first thing Bruster Cobb did was to build a steam powered, conveyer belt to carry buckets of water up and out of the mine. This kept the water level down to a depth of approximately 100 feet [30.5 m]. The next thing he did was to build a floor 25 feet [7.6 m] above the water line. That would be the main floor of the facility. Later, there was a joke that Cobb's balloon ship was actually built on a lake. Since the only entrance was from the roof, 12 funiculars were built for hauling workers and material. Six funiculars had cranes built into them. As a safety measure, Travis Cobb had several lifeboats mounted on the walls near the bottom floor. He reasoned that in the event of a flood, workers could use them to float up to escape exits in the roof. Is spite of being laughed at, his concern proved insightful early during the hanger's construction. Just two months after construction began, central Texas was hit by several torrential storms, and the crater flooded to 70 feet [21.3m] above the hanger floor. 130 workers floated to safety.

Having construction very similar to a sailing ship, Minerva's hull was built at a shipyard on Galveston Island. Upon completion, it was transported to Waco by a special steam train. The Cobbs felt a sense of the future as they watched the ship's hull lowered into the mine by a balloon crane. Once Minerva's hull was in place the true assembly work could begin. At this point Bruster Cobb started to feel the project was going to open doors to the future. He began to focus his entire time on the ship. Travis Cobb began to wonder at the magnitude of the project. As expected, there were cost overruns. His accountants were getting nervous. Every time he was called into a meeting he wondered "Oh God, what is it this time!" Just prior to the ship's completion he actually began to quietly regret his decision.

33. **A SECOND TORRENTIAL STORM** hit the Waco area prior to the balloon ship's arrival. As before, the workers in Crater Hanger were able to reach safety using lifeboats. The dome was opened after the storm and the hanger crew worked to repair flood damage.

34. **THE BALLOON SHIP'S HULL** was built at a shipyard on Galveston Island. Bruster Cobb and Diana Raleigh made frequent trips down to Galveston to oversee the progress.

35. **A GRAND DUAL RAIL LINE** that ran the 235 miles [378 km] between Galveston and Waco had to be constructed for a special flat car that was large enough to carry the balloon ship's hull. The single car was pulled by two steam engines on each track. Both the hull and all four engines were struck several times by lightning on the route to Waco.

36. **OVERSEEING THE EVENT FROM** an observation balloon, both Bruster Cobb and Diana Raleigh watch as the balloon ship's hull is lowered into Crater Hanger by balloon crane.

37. **A SHIP UNLIKE ANY OTHER** begins to take shape at Crater Hanger. As the ship's massive balloon ring is hoisted into place, both Cobb and Raleigh began to get a true sense of the ship's actual size. The buildings and wine cellar before them gave Bruster the impression that the ship was going to be more like a small town.

38. **LOOKING OUT FROM A NEARBY FUNICULAR** with a quiet disdain, Bruster Cobb watches as the large rooster is inflated on top of the soon to be completed balloon ship.

On March 13, 1555, the newly completed balloon ship was christened "Minerva", after Minerva Jane Cobb. Because the ship was named after her, Minerva Cobb was given the honor of smashing the champagne bottle against the ship's hull. It was an unusual ceremony. Instead of the ship launching out into the water like most ships do, this one slowly rose up overhead into the sky. It was an impressive sight. Everyone standing down on the hanger's bottom floor could hear the cheers from all around above as the ship floated high up on its first test flight. Cobb, Raleigh, and a select crew of 20 began flight tests. The initial crew was to be 50. After test flights began, news of the ship began to spread.

Volunteers came from all around. Cobb was approached by one person he never expected to hear from, his old commanding officer, Lieutenant Dorner. He had a young nephew, Donald Hadley, who had balloon experience and wanted to join Minerva's crew. He asked his uncle to come on his behalf. At first Cobb wasn't sure what to think, but if young Hadley was anything like his uncle, he would be an asset. Cobb remembered his personality clashed with Dorner's at times, but on a personal level he always respected Dorner. He wondered if any of his general ballooning skills rubbed off on his young nephew. Cobb hired Hadley to be a rigger. By April 20 all crew members had been chosen.

During the test flights the newly assembled crew learned to work together. Both Cobb and Raleigh were surprised to learn there was more to Hermes than previously thought. On three occasions he warned them of bad weather before it came to pass. And on another occasion, he warned of rigging failure before it happened. Because of the special circumstances surrounding his selection, a small cabin near the helm that was originally intended for storage was converted into his sleeping quarters. Bruster made sure it also had a drawing table with everything needed so Hermes could continue with his artwork. After several flight tests Cobb and Raleigh discovered more of Hermes watercolors. Some were of the ship, some of the Texas skyline, and some of crew members. They had the look of being done by a highly skilled artist. It turned out Hermes had a photographic memory. Cobb decided to have him carefully illustrate and document all the newly discovered plant life they hoped to encounter. Over the next several weeks the flight tests continued. Both Cobb and Raleigh wanted to launch before June.

39. **THE INITIAL LAUNCH** of the Minerva on its first test flight was an impressive sight as the completed ship came out in the full light of day for the first time.

1869, Lionheart Castle, Arizona

Upon his return to Earth, after making his historic interstellar voyage, Lionheart was a changed man. Even his longtime friend, Margret Dana noticed a difference. He was going back to the stars, possibly to stay. To the surprise of everyone, less than a month later Lionheart ordered the starship Elizabeth dismantled. Her parts would be needed for a new ship he had in mind. In July 1869, Lionheart gave a formal presentation of his plans for a new ship. It was unlike anything anyone had ever seen or imagined. It didn't look like a ship at all but more like an old gothic tower. To Lionheart's mind this new ship would be a doorway to other worlds. He would call it "The Onyx Tower". During his first interstellar voyage, Lionheart would have explored further if he had the means. This new ship would be large enough to house several smaller vehicles that would allow for further exploration of any environment whatever it might be. It also contained a factory that would fabricate almost anything if the raw materials are available. Lionheart had evidence there would be.

The new ship would have a crew of 400. In addition to everything else, Lionheart wanted to have the option of starting a human colony in another star system. As construction began, it was rumored he was building an arc to ferry humans to the stars. The basic shape of the new ship was like a cube with a cylinder rising out of the top. The height, width, and depth of the cube measured approximately 300 feet [91.3m]. The cylindrical tower feature on the top gave the ship a total height of 586 feet [178.6m].

Lionheart's Onyx Tower took 8 years to build, and its construction completely exhausted all of his resources. His last remaining Arizona property, including the Dark Castle, was sold to his longtime friend Margret Dana who was now one of the wealthiest people in the world with the advent of her internal drive engine. During the years of the Onyx Tower's construction, and the two years of flight tests that followed, Lionheart made arrangements for crew selection. All were told there was a possibility they would not return to Earth. In spite of that fact, there were many volunteers and all of them had read Lionheart's "Astro Voyage" book (based on the Elizabeth voyage) and wanted a chance to live the adventure.

40. LIONHEART'S INSPIRATION for the Onyx Tower was based on an old illustration taken from a children's book written centuries earlier. Lionheart was a complex man with powerful forces at work inside of him. He imagined a flying castle that could reach distant worlds, light years away. It was to be a ship like no other.

41. THE ONYX TOWER BEGINS TO RISE as builders work around the clock on Lionheart's grand starship. Unknown to most everyone, Lionheart's cancer was advancing. He knew he didn't have that much longer to live. He hoped the ship would be finished in time for him to leave. Lionheart wanted to die among the stars.

Tragically, on July 20, 1879, just six months before the Onyx Tower's planned departure, Peter Edward Lionheart passed away. He was 71 years old. Lionheart had been battling cancer. The funeral was a small gathering with only a few close family members. Lionheart left his entire fortune to his young nephew, Peter Markus Lionheart who was only 27 years old. Very little was known about him. He was determined to carry on his uncle's work.

Prior to his death, Peter Edward Lionheart was approached by John Powers Terra. Terra had perfected the science of life re-generation. Terra revealed he had already gone through the process three times, meaning he was now living in his 4th body. Lionheart was cordial with Terra at first, but he wanted to investigate Terra before accepting the invite. A background check revealed very little about John Terra. His grandfather, Powers Terra, was a different story. There were many horror stories surrounding the name of Powers Terra. He was said to be a mad scientist that experimented by creating deadly plant life forms that terrorized a village in Norway. Many people were killed. The only thing Lionheart could find out about John Terra was that he was one of the leading researchers in life sciences. Faced with certain death from cancer, Lionheart accepted Terra's invitation. Knowing that his cancer would become fatal very soon, Lionheart fell out of the public eye while he was taken to a place Terra called Gilgamesh Island to undergo the procedure. After that Peter Edward Lionheart became Peter Markus Lionheart. Terra revealed to Lionheart that he was having thoughts of creating an Immortals Club. Terra believed humanity might benefit from gifted individuals of they could live beyond their years. Lionheart said it could also be a horrible curse if it fell into the wrong hands.

Young Peter Markus Lionheart had an extensive itinerary planned for the Onyx Tower. He planned to visit Proxima b in the Alpha Centauri system, then continue on to Barnard's Star, 61 Cygni 2, Tau Ceti, Epsilon Endi, and Sirius 2. He also made arrangements to send messages back to Earth from time-to-time reporting discoveries, etc. Dana agreed to set up a listening post to receive his messages even though it would take several years to receive them. On January 24, 1880, the Onyx Tower lifted off from Lionheart airfield. Moments later it flew near the Dark Castle before ascending up into space. Spectators on the ground were somewhat taken back by the sight. In some ways the ship was like a flying mountain.

42. **WHEN LIONHEART AWOKE** in the isolation chamber on Gilgamesh Island, a skeleton was all that remained of his original body. His mind with all its memories was fully intact. His new body was much stronger, but it was no longer completely human. He was now a plant-animal hybrid. Terra told him he would have to repeat the procedure in 50 years. If not, the plant side of his nature would start to become more and more dominant.

43. **MARIE DANA MET WITH PETER MARKUS LIONHEART** one last time before the Onyx Tower departed. She gave Lionheart a book with a letter enclosed and told him not to open it until after departure. When he asked about it, she said "many years from now a much younger Margret Dana will come to the tower. You will know what to do. It is all explained in the letter enclosed." At that point they both realized the other had gone through Terra's re-generation process. Dana revealed that Terra formed the Immortals Club at the start of the new year.

44. JANUARY 24, 1880, before departing Earth, the Onyx Tower flies past Dana Castle (formerly the Dark Castle).

1555, Waco, Texas

May 5th, the Minerva lifted off from Waco, Texas on its maiden voyage. With a strong wind blowing to the south, the ship headed toward the Gulf. People came from all around to see the event. Many crewmembers waved back at their families as they departed. The wind blew the strongest in the desired direction at two thousand feet. Raleigh held the ship steady at that altitude. With Minerva's sails fully extended, she estimated they would reach the Gulf coast in four and a half hours. Later, as they approached the coast, Hermes came to the helm. He began to rock back and forth with a worried look on his face. Cobb and Raleigh became somewhat concerned, as the rocking motion was typical for Hermes before he warned them something bad was about to happen.

"After today, the Minerva will never again fly over Texas ", Hermes said as he stopped rocking. He became quiet again once they were out over water. Cobb and Raleigh looked at each other thinking Hermes gave warning the ship might not return from its first voyage. Had it not been for his accurate weather predictions during the flight test, they would have had less concern.

Five days into the voyage, they were still heading due south over water with no land in sight. It was hot and humid, even at a thousand feet up where there was still a slight southern breeze. For the first time since the battle of Wolf Pen, seven years earlier, a darker side of Cobb's personally was beginning to re-emerge. He wanted a drink. The heat made him thirsty, and a cold beer was all he could think about. The more he thought about it, the more the heat seemed excessive, even at low altitude. In spite of the fact that Cobb's family came from England, he never liked lukewarm beer. "If only there was a way to cool that wine cellar hanging below the ship," he thought. A moment later he came to the helm. In spite of Raleigh's objections, he gave the order to fly lower over the water. When Cobb felt it wasn't low enough, he took the helm and brought the ship lower, submerging the wine cellar underwater.

"There, that will cool the sprits in no time," Cobb said has he released the helm. Raleigh just rolled her eyes.

45. **ON MAY 5ᵀᴴ 1555 THE MINERVA BALLOONSHIP** flew over Cobb Castle before departing on its maiden voyage.

46. HAVING CLEARED THE TEXAS COAST, Minerva headed out over the Gulf of Mexico.

47. AGAINST RALEIGH'S ADVISE, Captain Cobb lowered the wine cellar below the waves to cool the brew.

1880, Lionheart's Second Life

The Onyx Tower was on its way to the stars. Lionheart looked out his cabin window to see the Earth and Moon getting smaller and smaller. Soon they would be reduced to points of light, like the surrounding stars. It had only been a few hours since departing from Earth. He felt this was the beginning of his second life. His true age would have been 72. Now having gone through Terra's re-generation process, he had the body of a 27-year-old. He was now Peter Markus Lionheart, the sole heir to the vast fortune of Peter Edward Lionheart. The Onyx Tower had a crew of 350. Only a select few on board knew his true identity.

Among them was Ms. West, the ship's Librarian. To Lionheart, she was one of the most interesting members of the crew, and the only one who could challenge him in a serious game of chess (outside of Margret Dana). Ms. West had the collective knowledge of several encyclopedias in her head and could quickly respond to any verbal question put to her. When necessary, she could go deeper into any subject to provide highly detailed information that could rival experts on the subject. In addition to that, she also had full knowledge of the ship and its systems. Hectra West was an exact replica of Hectra, the mechanical crew member on the first Mars mission back in 1762 (118 years earlier). When Lionheart studied the history of the Mars mission, he became fascinated with Hectra and wanted a replica of her on board. Lionheart also made sure she had a mind of her own and would let him know if he was out of line. That was probably the best thing he liked most about her. Hectra was completed two years before the Onyx Tower. She often advised him during the ship's construction. Lionheart had an ongoing interest in history. He often had long conversations with Hectra on the subject. As he continued to look out of his cabin window at the small Earth among the stars, he realized he was now seeing beyond his years.

48. HECTRA WEST was the ships Liberian and head Science Officer aboard the Onyx Tower. Lionheart built a close replica of the West android that was aboard the first manned Mars mission 118 years earlier.

49. **DURING THE CONSTRUCTION** of the Onyx Tower, Lionheart often engaged in an ongoing game of chess with West during breaks to relieve his mind from the day-to-day work.

There was a knock at the door of his cabin. It was Jane Connors, the head medical officer. "Pete, there is something I've wanted to ask you for some time," Connors said, breaking Lionheart's train of thought.

"What is it?" Lionheart asked, turning away from the window.

"I have always wondered about this ship, the Onyx Tower. Why did you build a starship to look like an old medieval castle?"

"Well..., Lionheart paused for a moment to take a deep breath. "That's very interesting. In all this time, except for Ms. West, you are the first one to ask me. I guess the initial thought of it came to me when I came across something while hiking long ago." Lionheart stopped for a moment then continued. "As far back as I can remember I have always had a fascination with the medieval period. Sometimes I wonder if I lived there in another life. When I was in college there was a game, I used to play that was set back in that same time period. In the game there was a mysterious tower called the Onyx Tower. It wasn't really a tower at all, but rather a gateway to other worlds, other places of existence. In a way I wanted this ship to be a doorway to other worlds, and I suppose in a way, the means to live out my fantasies," Lionheart said.

"Interesting. When I first heard that you were building a second starship, I imagined it would be similar to the Elizabeth," Connors said.

Before Lionheart could answer there was a beep from his intercom. "Yes, what is it?" he responded.

"Captain, please come to the Wardroom, there is something I think you need to see," came the voice of First Officer Thornton.

"I'm on my way," Lionheart said as he and Connors left his quarters.

Moments later they were in the Wardroom. In the center of the room was a round elevated electronic platform. Hovering above the platform was a semi-transparent projection of the 8th planet, Neptune. In the planet's northern hemisphere was a small yellow-orange glowing sphere. It would go away then reappear. Stepping up to the platform, Lionheart tried to get a better look at what was being projected.

"What exactly am I looking at?" Lionheart asked.

"That's just it sir, we don't know what it is," Thornton said stepping up. "At first we thought it might be some kind of static electric anomaly. Then we detected nitrogen and oxygen in its general proximity. But what caught our attention was the temperature inside the anomaly which is much warmer than the surrounding atmosphere. It is 32.9°F [0.5°C] inside the anomaly, far above the surrounding -353°F [-214°C], typical for Neptune. And that's not all...," Thornton paused for a moment. "In the area close in around the anomaly, the air is unusually calm, almost still, while the surrounding atmosphere has normal winds, currently blowing at 1287 miles [2071.2 kilometers] per hour, again typical for Neptune. The anomaly also appears to be phasing in and out. One minute it is there, the next it is not."

"Interesting, what would you suggest? Lionheart asked.

"Captain, if I may...," assistant science officer Andrews said interrupting. "I think we should definitely go in for a closer look sir. Right now, it will be at least three weeks before anyone else can get out here. And there is the distinct possibility the anomaly may be gone by then. From our current position we can reach Neptune in three days if we reverse the ships' engines. Captain, I know our mission is to explore the unknown of nearby interstellar space, but I think is a very unique opportunity, and it's in our own backyard."

"Captain, I would advise caution," West said entering the room. "I can't tell the exact nature of the anomaly from this distance, but the fact that it phases in and out troubles me."

"Why does it trouble you?" Lionheart asked.

"I can't give a specific answer until I have looked into it further, but from what little I can determine, the anomaly appears to have properties similar to little known energy experiments that were conducted many years ago."

"What kind of experiments?"

"They involved research into a particular aspect of inter-dimensional physics. Not long after beginning, they were considered too dangerous to continue and were shut down," West explained.

"What aspect are we talking about?" Lionheart asked.

"I can't say without closer observation. If you choose to investigate this, I would advise a cautious approach Captain".

"Captain, even if there is a possible danger, this is what we came out here for," Thornton said.

80

Everyone in the Wardroom became quiet as they waited for the Captain's answer.

"I agree. Set course for Neptune. West, send a message back to Dana on our situation and keep me updated on anything you observe."

"Of course, Captain." West responded.

50. **IN THE WARDROOM** of the Onyx Tower, (left to right) Lionheart, Conners, West and Thornton examine the unknown anomaly in Neptune's northern hemisphere.

1555, The Pirates

Approximately two hours after dragging the wine cellar through the sea, the Minerva started to gain altitude. Once all the sea water drained out of the wine cellar, Captain Cobb with crew members Ian and Marston, made their way down and returned to the main ship, each carrying two small casks strapped on their backs. The beer was cold and foamy, just the way Cobb liked it. The sun was going down. At the helm, Raleigh gave the order to gain and hold altitude at 2000 feet [609.6m]. She believed their position to be somewhere north of the Yucatan. There had been reports of pirates operating in the area. After a while, Cobb was under the influence and feeling no pain. As he looked out over the clouds from his cabin, he was reminded of all the times he drank while in the observation balloon during the war, when most of the time, his only companion was boredom. For a moment he thought he heard the distant crackle of cannon fire. He thought it was only his imagination at first. Then the sound came again. It was cannon fire! Still somewhat in a stupor, he got to his feet and made his way to the helm.

"Captain, a ship below has come under attack from pirates! We have to do something!" Raleigh said.

"This is not a warship, and we have to conserve our resources," Cobb responded.

"You can't be serious! I can't believe you would let this happen!" She said.

"It's not our fight!" Cobb said as he headed back to his cabin.

"Marston, steer the ship to pass directly over the pirates," She commanded.

"But commander! The Captain said...," Marston responded.

"Never mind what the Captain said! I'm in command when he is off the bridge!" Marston changed course to pass directly over what was happening below.

"What is going on?" Hadley asked as he came up from behind.

"Hadley, Come with me!" Raleigh commanded.

A moment later, Raleigh and Hadley were in the ship's stores. They came back out on deck carrying a small kerosene flask with a rag attached to it. Raleigh lit the rag just as Hadley tossed it out from the front of the ship. It struck the attacking pirate ship below, but the rag blew out. The Pirates, now alerted to Minerva, began shooting upward.

"You will never get them that way!" Cobb shouted, as has he ran out on deck. Using the bridge harpoon gun, he fired an anchor line that struck and latched on to the center mast of the pirate ship. It held. Minerva swung around violently. Holding another kerosene flask, Cobb slid down on a line to the wine cellar's catwalk. Bullets from the pirate ship hit the boards under his feet as he danced his way to the cellar entrance. Coming out a moment later, he lit the rag attached to a cask he was holding. As he waited for the gunfire below to ease, the rag began to burn dangerously close to the cask. Seeing what was happening from above, Raleigh and three other crewmen began firing at the pirates below. In the brief moment the pirates stopped shooting at Cobb, he threw the cask. It exploded when it hit the deck of the ship below. Seconds later there was a grand explosion that blew the pirate ship apart. Cobb stumbled back onto the wine cellar. Even though the harpoon line was now dangling with only a piece of the pirate's top mast attached, Raleigh cut it to free from the Minerva. The remaining pieces of the pirate ship were on fire. Raleigh, Hadley, and the others watched as the remains of the Pirate ship sank into the sea. Minerva was drifting higher and higher.

"What happened? Why did the ship explode like that?" Marston asked.

"The fire from our bomb must have reached the ships magazine. Fortunately for us, we gained a lot of altitude before it went off, otherwise we might have caught fire also. Take the wheel. Hadley, come with me. I'm going to see if the Captain is alright," Raleigh said. They found Cobb lying on the floor of the wine cellar. It turned out he had passed out from drinking too much.

"How is it possible the Captain could have done all of that while being drunk?" Hadley asked.

"As long as I've known him, he has always been that way. He seems to hold his liquor better than anyone, and then suddenly, it hits him. Come on, help me get him back to his cabin," Raleigh said.

51. CAPTAIN BRUSTER TEX COBB of the Minerva balloon ship.

52. THE NEXT MORNING Raleigh's notion was confirmed. Sometime during the night, they passed over the northern Yucatan coast and were now over dense jungle. Off in the horizon Raleigh could see the tops of pyramids rising out of the foliage.

"Commander, the Captain wants you to report to his Quarters." Marston said.

"Well, I knew he would want to see me sooner or later," Raleigh said, as she left the bridge.

Later in Cobb's cabin, they had the heated discussion she was waiting for. She saved a cargo ship and its crew, sank a pirate ship, but disobeyed a direct order from the Captain. Deep down Cobb knew there really was little he could do about it. James Raleigh was the largest investor in the ship. Without his backing the venture never would have been possible. Cobb also knew his daughter would be too head strong and possibly hard to control. In an effort to at least appear in control he ended the conversation with "Don't ever do that again." Cobb's head was still ringing from a bad hangover. When Raleigh yelled back at him, his head pounded, and she knew it.

Cobb slowly made his way to the bridge a few hours later. Seeing the pyramids, Robert Malvern insisted on landing the ship so he could collect plant samples. Before a slightly hungover Captain Cobb could reply, Raleigh advised against it. Like America, there were still several areas in Mexico that were not under any kind of civilized authority and therefore not subject to any laws. Some of the local natives were known to offer up visitors as human sacrifices. Cobb agreed it was too dangerous. "If we have seen their pyramids, it's a sure bet, they have seen us. No, It's too dangerous".

By now, everyone on board knew of the slight rift between the Captain and the first officer. Malvern hoped the Captain would see things his way. By afternoon they were over dense jungle again. There was no sign of any kind of settlement below, at least as far as anyone could tell. It was decided that this might be a good place to look for exotic plants. The order was given to drop anchor. Hermes Butchart came out on deck and looked out over the dense jungle below. "It's not safe here. There is something down there, and it is very hungry." He stepped away from the rail and returned to his cabin. After he left everyone paused for a moment.

53. **"IT'S NOT SAFE HERE.** There is something down there and it is very hungry." Hermes Bushart warned Captain Cobb before sending a landing party down into the dense rain forest below.

A few minutes later, Cobb, Malvern, Hadley, Marston, and Ian, entered the ship's elevator cage and were lowered down to a small clearing below. At first, they were somewhat startled by the animal sounds coming from all around. Then, using scimitars, they cautiously made their way into the dense jungle. It wasn't long until Cobb and Malvern had collected several plant samples. Everyone was amazed by large colorful birds all around. After a short time, the birds all suddenly flew off for some unknown reason. It frightened Cobb at first, but like the others he continued the search for exotic plants. Leaning over, Malvern was about to dig up a small specimen when he noticed something unusual about the shadow of the tree he was under. It moved! Still kneeling down he slowly stood up. As he did so he began to feel the hot breath above him. Looking up slowly, he saw the tree above was actually a giant snake that was about to strike. Before he could cry out, the beast reached down and seized him from the waist up! Snapping its head back it proceeded to swallow him whole! Terrified by what was happening, the other party members began to hack away at the beast with little effect. There was little they could do to fend off the monster. Then, without warning, a rain of small arrows came out of the forest from all directions, striking the snake. Cobb and the others ducked down to avoid being struck themselves. The penetrating arrows had no effect on the beast at first. Seconds later, it began to slowly sway back and forth as it came under the influence of the poison arrows. No longer able to hold its head up, the snake fell to the ground completely unconscious. Cobb and the others slowly stood up. It was clear they were not alone.

The jungle was suddenly silent. Slowly, Cobb and the others looked out all around. The jungle itself started moving. Native Indians appeared from every direction. It was as though they had always been there but invisible. Cobb and the others were surrounded and forced to move away from the beast. Several Indians flipped the beast over and began to cut into its underside. Within a minute or two, Malvern was pulled out still alive! Cobb's landing party was taken prisoner and escorted away. Up in the Minerva, Raleigh pulled the cage up to bring down more reinforcements, but the line had been cut. The jungle was so thick no one could be seen below. Even the landing cage had vanished.

54. THE BEAST CAME UPON THE LANGING PARTY before anyone could react. As their landing party came under attack, Captain Cobb and the others began to hack away at the beast with little effect.

A second smaller cage was lowered down to just above the treetops. It carried crewman Hardman. He tried to survey the area below as best he could. He could just see several natives below carving up the remains of the giant snake. They seemed completely unaware of his presence. There was still no sign of the landing party or the cage they came down in. After receiving the report from Hardman, Raleigh decided to take the Minerva back to the general area of the pyramids. As a balloon ship, the Minerva had very poor directional control, especially against the wind, but over the right landscape it had the ability to line walk. It is a process where a small anchor (with retractable spikes) is fired from the forward harpoon gun to catch on some rocks or trees below. The line is slowly pulled in until the ship is almost directly overhead. Another line is fired and catches in an area up ahead. The anchor directly below releases its hold and is pulled up. Then the forward line in pulled in until the ship is overhead again. Line walking is a slow process, but under the right conditions the ship can slowly move against the wind, if it's not too strong.

The line walking was slow going at best. Once a large snake tried to hitch a ride on an anchor being pulled back to the ship. That gave Raleigh an idea. The snake was pulled onto the deck, and it took five crewmen to bind it into a gunny sack. The sun was going down and a slight wind was coming up behind them. Raleigh gave the order to stop line walking. Later in the darkness of a clear moonless night the faint orange glow of small fires off in the horizon near the pyramids could be seen. As luck would have it, there was a slight breeze moving the Minerva in that direction. When Minerva got closer, Raleigh and the others could see and hear some kind of ceremony taking place at the top of one pyramid. Moving in closer, they could see Minerva's cage with the landing party enclosed. The natives had dragged it up to the top of the pyramid. Some kind of ritual was taking place. Based on what Raleigh heard about the local natives, she believed it was going to be a sacrifice. The natives opened the cage door and started to pull Hadley out. Cobb lunged forward to fight them off but was forced back by several natives jabbing him with spears. Bruised and bloodied, Cobb fell back in the cage. Hadley was dragged out and held over an altar stone.

"When I give the order, drop the anchor line as close to the cage as you can get," Raleigh commanded, as they got closer. She carefully steered the ship so it would pass directly overhead.

"Now!" she commanded. The large snake was dumped over the high priests standing near the altar stone. At that same moment the anchor snagged the landing cage, and started to pull it across the pyramid top with the landing party in it. In the chaos and frenzy, Hadley jumped off the altar stone, ran over, and grabbed on to the cage as it passed by. Cobb and the others reached out and grabbed on to Hadley as best as they could. The cage swung back and forth as it cleared the pyramid's top. As the ship continued to move away from the area, the cage was slowly pulled up. Soon they were back over the jungle again.

They managed to get away, but it was not without losing crewmen Ian, who had been impaled by a spear as the cage was rising. Cobb had several small puncture wounds and had passed out. As Minerva ascended, arrows were thrown but the natives stopped when they started falling back on their people at the pyramid's base. Later when Cobb woke up in his bunk, he saw someone had bandaged him up. For the first time he was glad to have Raleigh as his second. In spite of his mild distain for her, he knew the ship would be in capable hands. The wind was taking them east out over the Atlantic.

1880, Neptune

Three days after Lionheart gave the order, the Onyx Tower reached Neptune. Using its internal drive engine to offset Neptune's gravity, the Onyx Tower hovered in space above the anomaly. Lionheart was very unsettled, and it wasn't from his ship hovering above an unknown anomaly near a gas giant. It was because Ms. West had to be taken offline just before she was to report her latest observation. During her charging cycle, a power surge shorted out some of her systems. Shortly after, Chief Engineer Petrov quietly reported to Lionheart her charging system may have been tampered with. She could be completely restored, but not before the ship reached Neptune. Lionheart was called to the wardroom.

"Captain, the anomaly is 1000 miles [1609.4 kilometers] below us," Thornton said.

"Very good. Take us down. Let's get a closer look," Lionheart command.

Moments later, the Onyx Tower hovered just a few miles away from the anomaly. Science officer Andrews and his team began making their close observations.

"Captain, we are going to launch a probe," Andrews announced.

Moments later, a small spherical probe shot away from the ship. As it flew out, it fired small thrusters correcting its direction. From the wardroom everyone watched the screen that showed what the probe's camera was seeing as it flew into the heart of the anomaly. At first, they saw only the blinding light from the anomalies' core, then a different scene appeared, one that no one expected. For a brief second, it looked like somewhere on Earth. The landscape looked like rolling green tundra. Then the screen looked like it was suddenly iced over and then all contact with the probe was lost.

"What the hell was that?" Thornton quietly asked himself.

"I don't know," Lionheart said.

Andrews didn't say anything. His team began replaying the recording over and over. A strange feeling began to overtake Lionheart. He wanted input from West. He went down to Engineering. When he got there, he saw Petrov working on West. Lying back on an inclined table, West looked like she was powered up but not conscious.

"I'm almost finished with her, Captain," Petrov said, as Lionheart entered.

55. **THE ONYX TOWER** held position several miles above the anomaly as it hovered in the upper atmosphere of Neptune.

"Was there any permanent damage, any permanent memory loss?" Lionheart asked.

"Nothing that can't be easily restored. In addition to her latest observation, taken twenty hours ago, I've also uploaded the results from Andrew's probe. She will be completely updated when she awakens," Petrov said.

"Ok, nice work Petrov," Lionheart said, as he left Engineering. Moments later, on one of the ship's observation decks, he watched many others observing the unusual grand event below. At first glance, Lionheart didn't know which sight was more overwhelming, the anomaly itself or the wide endless expanse of Neptune's blue horizon. He still had the strangest feeling about the anomaly. He began to feel he had seen it somewhere before, but where? He was reminded of something, but what? Lionheart returned to his quarters.

"Captain, Ms. West is awake," Petrov said, over the com.

"I'll be right there," Lionheart said, as he rushed out. When he arrived back in Engineering, he saw West getting up off the table. Before he could speak, she interrupted him.

"Captain, there is a danger. We must leave here at once!" she said.

"Commander Thornton, Lionheart here, take us out of the area. I don't want to be any closer than 100,000 miles [160,935 kilometers] from this thing. Do it now!" Lionheart said, into his intercom.

"Aye, Captain, but Andrews and the science team has not yet finished their observation," Thornton responded.

"Never mind about that, just get the ship out of here now!" Lionheart commanded, as he and West headed for the Bridge. A moment later, they were alone in the elevator.

"Captain, there is something else," West said.

"What is it?"

"In our communication with Dana back on Earth, I have detected a second signal buried within. It first appeared only as background static, but it is a definite signal. Someone on this ship is sending messages to Dana or someone who is working close with Dana." West said.

Standing in the elevator, Lionheart began to feel his weight increasing as the ship began to move away from the anomaly. Per Lionheart's orders, the Onyx Tower started moving up from Neptune's upper atmosphere into space. Down below, the anomaly continued to phase in and out, just as it had been, then it phased out and was gone.

"Captain, the anomaly appears to have phased out completely. It's gone Sir. Should we resume a hover position?" Thornton asked.

"Captain, we are still in proximity of danger. We must get further away," West said before Lionheart could respond.

"No, Mr. Thornton. Let's move the tower away from here. Increase to full," Lionheart said then switched to the ships main com. "This is the Captain; everyone brace for maximum acceleration!"

Everyone all over the ship got down on the floor or wherever they could lie down. As the internal drive engine came to full power, the gravity rose to three G's. At first it seemed the Onyx Tower was out of danger, then the anomaly phased back in, directly ahead of them. There was no time to react. The ship was swallowed up by the anomaly. At first there was a blinding light all around the ship. At the same time the internal drive engine shut down. For a brief moment everyone became weightless as the ship went to zero G. As the engine came back online, the ship was once again back to one G only. Lionheart quickly got to his feet. A crackling sound was coming from outside all around the ship. Suddenly, every window and external camera lens iced over. No one could see outside the ship. The internal drive began to shut down again. Ships sensors indicated that they were at an altitude of 50,000 feet [15240m] above a planet with a mass the same as Earth and descending at a rate of 100 feet [30.5m] per second. The ship started to rock back and forth as it fell.

"Petrov, we have less than a minute to get the internal drive engine back online!" Thornton said yelling into the com.

"Aye Thornton, we are going the best we can! When we passed through that anomaly back there, it overloaded the engine circuit breakers! It will take at least two minutes to replace them!" Petrov said.

"Petrov, we don't have two minutes! Thornton, come with me! There might be a way we can slow our decent," Lionheart said.

"Do you mean the solar sail?" Thornton asked.

"It's our only hope," Lionheart said, as they entered a nearby control room. Lionheart stood near a large handle. Thornton stood near another on the far side of the room.

"Ready, Now!" Lionheart said as they both pulled the large handles at the same time. Several large, bundled sails shot out from the upper tower. Within seconds they unfurled in the frigid wind, forming a grand parachute above the tower. There was a jolt as they fully deployed, causing several crew to fall to the floor as the ship suddenly slowed its descent. Thornton and Lionheart got back to their feet and ran back to the bridge.

"The ship is slowing, Captain. Our rate of decent is now 30 feet [9.1 meters] per second. Impact will be in seventeen minutes, twenty-seven-seconds," Thornton said.

"Petrov, how is it coming down there?" Lionheart asked.

"We are about halfway done Captain."

Some of the ice had broken away from the windows.

"Captain, it looks like we were over the Earth, but I have no idea where," Helmsmen Quinn responded.

Lionheart took a deep breath. Suddenly under the strain of the ship's weight, the solar sail tore away. They were in free fall again.

"Petrov!" Lionheart said.

"Almost there Captain!"

"Impact in Twenty-Seconds; Nineteen, Eighteen, Seventeen...," Thornton said, as he counted down in calm voice.

"Ten, Nine, Eight...," Thornton continued.

Suddenly, the sound of the internal drive engine could be heard. Everyone became heavy as the ship's descent slowed to a stop. It now hovered just a hundred feet above the water.

"Petrov, you just saved us all. Mr. Thornton, Take us up to 200,000 feet [60960 meters] and hold position. We need to find out exactly where we are." Lionheart said.

"Captain, there is a problem with the Dana engine. We have to land as soon as we can!" Petrov responded.

"Captain, ship's sensors are working again. We appear to be over a large lake, and the anomaly we just passed through is not far away, but appears to be fading," Andrews reported.

"Very well, set us down on the lake and hold position." Lionheart commanded.

Just as the ship started to touch down in the water, the internal drive engine went offline again. The ship violently shifted to one side as it splashed down in the lake. Still covered in ice, the Onyx Tower looked like a floating winter castle.

"We need to find out where we are. Mr. Thornton, launch a rocket probe, trim all ballast, submerge the ship. I want to try to conceal our presence here until we know our location," Lionheart commanded.

A small rocket fired out from the tower's roof and disappeared into the thick clouds above. As bubbles of air rushed out from the ballast tanks, the castle of ice slowly sank into the lake. Big chunks of ice started to break off into the surrounding water as the tower sank. Each time a chunk of ice broke off there was a loud clap of thunder, like ice breaking away from a glacier.

"Where did the ice around the ship come from?" Helmsmen Anders asked.

"Condensation Mr. Anders. The temperature back on Neptune is over 350 degrees below zero Fahrenheit, 380 degrees cooler then it is outside here on Earth-, if this is the Earth. When we passed through that portal or whatever it was, the outside of the ship froze instantly," Thornton answered.

Everyone felt a quiet thump as the ship came to rest at the bottom of the lake. The upper tower dome was still above the water line.

56. **WITH IT'S INTERNAL ENGINE OFFLINE,** the Onyx Tower violently plunged into the lake.

"Captain, part of the ship is still visible. If there is anyone around the lake, they can see the upper dome," Thornton said.

"Captain, you need to come up here," Petrov said.

"What is it Petrov?" Lionheart responded.

"Sir, its better if you come up here, there is something I want you to see."

"I'm on my way," Lionheart responded as he and Thornton left the bridge. A moment later they were in the upper tower near the internal drive engine.

"Ok Petrov, what is this all about?" Lionheart asked.

"It's the circuit breakers on the Dana Engine. When we pulled them out, all eight of them were bad. Just before we left, they were closely inspected. I inspected them myself, and all of them were in perfect condition. They were designed and built to last several years. There is no way all of them could have gone bad. It's just not possible. And to make matters worse, there is no way the replacements could have gone bad just after putting them in!" Petrov said.

"What are you suggesting Petrov?" Lionheart said.

"Sir, we have a saboteur on board. There is no question about it," Petrov said.

"About the fuses, have they all been tampered with?" Thornton asked.

"I'm having them checked now by someone I trust."

"Petrov, if all of them are bad or have been tampered with, do we have the means to repair them?" Lionheart asked.

"Aye, I think so, but they won't be as reliable. I'm afraid if the saboteur can get to the Dana engine, there are other parts of the ship that could be much more catastrophic," Petrov said.

"The space distortion shells...," Lionheart said quietly.

"Precisely Sir," Petrov answered.

"Mr. Thornton, post security at all critical parts of the ship, but do it quietly. I don't want to alert our saboteur. I'll be in my quarters," Lionheart said.

57. **LIONHEART LOOKED OUT THE WINDOW** at the dark underwater view from his quarters. There was very little light from above. Occasionally, a fish would swim pass his window. The light from his cabin window attracted them. When he left Earth only a few weeks earlier, he never imagined ending up in the bottom of a deep lake.

There was a knock at the door. Lionheart expected to see Ms. West. She was directly tied into the ships' systems. He was certain she would have something to report. It was Thornton. Judging by the look on his face, Lionheart wondered if the situation could get any worse.

"Captain, we have received the report from our probe and now know our location," Thornton said.

"So, exactly where are we? Are we on Earth?" Lionheart asked.

"Yes, we are literally out in the middle of nowhere in Northwestern Siberia, and the lake we are in is unknown. It's not on any map. It is manmade. We are actually in a river valley. There is a dam approximately five miles to the south," Thornton said.

"Well judging by the look on your face when you first came in, I thought you would have something worse or profound to tell me," Lionheart said.

"There is more, and this is where it gets interesting. According to the ships elapsed time, we are only seventeen days into the voyage. We departed Earth on January 24, 1880, so today's date should be February 10, 1880."

"Go on," Lionheart said.

"When our probe flew into the upper atmosphere to get a better view of our location, it noticed that the Moon was in the wrong position for that date. That prompted the probe to check visible planet and star positions," Thornton said.

"Go on," Lionheart repeated slowly, as he sat down at his desk.

"According to the probe, the Moon, planets, and stars are in the position they would have been for July 13, 1627. When we first received the information, we had the probe run a self-diagnostic before falling back to Earth. It's last report was that its systems were nominal," Thornton said.

"So, if what you're telling me is true, that anomaly we passed thru not only displaced us by three billion miles, but also by approximately two and a half centuries," Lionheart stopped for a moment as he went into deep thought, leaning back in his chair. "Many years ago, back in the 1830's, Margret Dana was conducting experiments in what she called Inter-dimensional Physics." Lionheart continued. "Before discovering the basic principles that lead to developing the internal drive engine, she experimented with opening doorways that would allow an object to travel across great distances almost instantaneously."

"I recall reading about these experiments. I believe it was referred to as the Portal Project," Thornton said.

"As she got deeper into her work, she discovered if certain parameters were altered the doorway would not only allow passage through space, but time as well. As I remember, Dana was excited by the idea at first because, if perfected, it could allow travel through the universe in real time."

"How do you know all this?" Thornton asked.

"I backed her research, at least a good part of it. As the research continued, it turned out the parameters that influence time change where too difficult to control. Also, the possibility of being able to change the past was considered too dangerous, so that aspect of the experiments was discontinued. She told me she destroyed her notes and all other material relating to time travel. It just now suddenly dawned on me what it was about the anomaly that made me feel uneasy. I remember seeing a much smaller version of it in Dana's laboratory many years ago. I think that is what Ms. West was trying to warn me about. I wonder where she is. It's not like her to not be around when so much is going on," Lionheart said.

"Knowing Ms. West, I suspect she's in the middle of solving a problem that she will report to us shortly. You said you backed part of Dana's work. Do you know who the other backers were? Do you think they might have continued with the work she started, that was considered too dangerous?" Thornton asked.

"It's possible there might have been one that I can think of. I don't know too much about him. I remember him only as Dr. Serco. He was one of those eccentric billionaires that stayed out of the public eye. I never saw much of him and as I recall, and as far as I know, Dana told me she met with him only very rarely after he told her he wanted to back her research. You know if I didn't know better… "

"Captain Lionheart!" security officer Larson called out over the com.

"Lionheart here, what is it Larson?"

"Captain someone is stealing one of the amphibians!" Larson said.

Lionheart and Thornton rushed to the window and looked down. They could see the amphibian moving out away from the ship in the dark water below. Minutes later Lionheart and Thornton were down in the launch bay. The bay doors were closed, and the water had been pumped out. Petrov and two of his men were there. The moment Lionheart and Thornton arrived; Petrov led them off to a private area.

"How does someone steal a small research vehicle out of the bay without being seen?" Lionheart asked.

"Captain, right after the amphibian left the ship we found the bodies of Barnes, Sever, and Parker," Petrov said in a quiet voice.

"Three crew dead. What the hell is going on?" Lionheart asked himself in a quiet voice with anger.

"That's not all Captain, crewman Johnson and Science Officer Andrews are missing!" Petrov said.

"Mr. Petrov, we just found this," Larson said as he approached.

"What is it?" Thornton asked.

"It's a signal transponder taken from Ms. West. This means they have her. After I revived Ms. West before all the commotion, I told her to return in an hour so I could run another diagnostic. When things calmed down after we first came here, I sent for her. She said she would come back right after she helped Andrews and Johnson with a problem they were having in the launch bay. After a short time, I sent for her again. There was no reply, so I tried to contact Andrews and Johnson. When I didn't hear from them, I headed for the launch bay. That was when Larson announced one of the amphibians was leaving the ship. By the time I arrived, Larson found the bodies and West, Johnson and Andrews were missing," Petrov said.

"We have to find them, Fast! If Ms. West is compromised...," Lionheart said quietly.

"...whoever had her would know everything about this ship and the science behind it," Thornton said, finishing the sentence.

"Captain, I know this is highly unlikely, but you don't suppose that Ms. West...?" Thornton asked.

"I could never believe that. I had her programmed to be honest, strong minded, and even stand up to me, but not a murderer!" Lionheart said.

"Let's hope so. After all she has the strength of five men. She could easily... "

"I could never believe that!" Lionheart said interrupting. "Mr. Petrov, ready a second amphibian. We are going after them."

"Aye Sir," Petrov responded.

Forty minutes later, the launch bay flooded, and its doors opened. Shortly after, a heavily armed party of six led by Lionheart and Thornton launched in another amphibian. After a search all around the lake that lasted seventeen hours they finally caught up with the stolen amphibian. It was empty and the bodies of Andrews and Johnson were discovered nearby. They both had bloody open wounds all over their bodies and foam coming out of their nose and mouth. Thornton got down on one knee to examine the bodies more closely. Lionheart was somewhat disgusted by the sight.

"They're dead, Pete," Thornton said.

"What the devil could have done this?" Lionheart asked.

"I don't know. I've never seen anything like it. These look like sting wounds from a wasp or scorpion, but much larger. Whatever did this must have been a nightmare," Thornton said, getting back to his feet.

"There is no sign of Ms. West, and it looks like whatever killed Andrews and Johnson and also attacked the amphibian as well," Crewman Moss said. They looked over the vehicle. It had scratches all over its body as though whatever attacked was trying to sting its metal body. Some of the windows were broken out. The inside looked shredded.

"So, it was Andrews and Johnson that sabotaged the fuses, and Andrews was so eager for us to stop at Neptune, but why? If Petrov hadn't repaired those fuses in time, we would all be dead now and the ship would have been scattered across the land for miles. Why would they do this? Why would they attempt a suicide mission?" Lionheart asked.

"If the memory core in Ms. West was the intended goal, chances are it would have survived the crash," Thornton said.

"If the ship had crashed, whoever was waiting could simply search the area until they found what they were looking for, but when we landed safely, Andrews and Johnson had to go to plan "B" and get Ms. West off the ship. Right before we went through the anomaly West told me several hidden signals from Earth were sent to and from the ship," Lionheart said.

"Was she able to de-code them?" Thornton asked.

"No, she didn't have time before all the commotion started."

"Sir, there are other tracks here left by someone else. I can't say for sure, but it looks like they came here after the attack," Crewman Elston said.

"Yes, there are also wheel tracks here. It looks like whoever it was, they loaded West on a wagon, than pulled it off in that direction," Thornton said.

"Let's find out where." Lionheart said as they got back into their vehicle and followed the tracks. They led them through some rolling hills to what looked like a shallow river valley. The wagon trail ended on the valley floor near some tracks that were left behind by a much larger vehicle. Lionheart got out to get a closer look.

"Captain, whatever was here was very big and very heavy," Thornton said, as he knelt down to get a closer look.

"Land steamer?" Lionheart said.

"Judging by the size and depth of these tracks, it certainly looks that way Sir," Thornton said, getting back to his feet.

"They were around in the early 1600's; no doubt the Russians had them as well. I can't help but wonder who could have gotten to Andrews and Johnson. I trusted them completely," Lionheart said as he paused for a moment. "All right let's get back to the ship. We all need some rest and I want to see if Petrov has made any progress repairing those fuses. If we can get the ship operational, we can use its sensors to locate West. What the hell is that?" Lionheart said pointing to what looked like a school of birds on the horizon.

"I don't know. Whatever they are, they are too big to be birds and they're headed this way. They look more like bats." Thornton said.

As the school of flying creatures got closer, everyone could see their green glowing eyes. They were like miniature lions with bat like wings and long tails.

"Elston, Moss!" Lionheart said.

Moss and Elston powered up and razed their electric rifles.

The flying creatures circled around Lionheart and his men at first, then they suddenly dove in to attack. Everyone except Moss and Elston squatted down. With their rifles up and their backs to each other, Moss and Elston opened fire. Emitting powerful bolts of lightning, the electric guns fried most of the creatures instantly. The survivors flew off to the south. As Lionheart slowly got to his feet, he and the others looked all around at the bodies of the roasted smoking creatures nearby. Looking closer everyone could see they had scorpion like stingers at the end of their tails.

"That was close! Thank God we had electric guns," Lionheart said.

"What do you think they are Captain?" Moss asked.

"I don't know. I've never seen anything like it. Try to find one that isn't burned too badly. We will take it back to Connors for examination," Lionheart said.

Later, when Lionheart's party arrived back in the launch bay, Petrov saw the dead creature (in clear wrapping) as Moss handed it out to Elston. At first Petrov looked puzzled, then a look of horror came over his face as he quietly said "Tiesposka-".

"Petrov, do you know what this is?" Lionheart asked.

"It is Russian folklore Captain. It is the legend of the Siberian Kings. Long ago there was a story of a hidden empire, a shadow empire that was located somewhere deep in western Siberia. According to the legend this empire was run by one of Czar Alexander's relatives, Count Vladislav. It was said that he ruled an incredible mining empire and built a fleet of subterranean steamships. As long as the ore flowed west to Moscow, he was allowed to run his empire without any interference. But also, according to the legend, he had an evil brother known only as Krnobov. It was said he conducted experiments on animals. The result was the creation of Tiesposka, or Death Cat. He hoped to use them as a battle weapon," Petrov said.

"You seem to know all about this legend Petrov," Thornton said.

"How did this legend end?" Lionheart asked.

"Apparently, it all ended in a violent slave revolt that destroyed everything. In the years that followed, several expeditions were mounted but they found no trace of Vladislav's empire," Petrov explained.

"Very interesting Petrov, Mr. Thornton, take this specimen to Connors. I'll be in my quarters," Lionheart said.

58. **THE CREATURE STILL SMOLDERED** as Dr. Connors started to examine it. Petrov was somewhat horrified from looking at a creature that was from stories he heard as a child.

1704, Aegean Sea

Standing at Minerva's helm with Hadley and Raleigh, Hermes started bobbing back and forth again. "A storm with many doorways is coming," Hermes said. He than left for his cabin. The next day they held a burial at sea for crewman Ian. Minerva flew lower to allow the wine cellar's catwalk to be just a foot above the calm water. After crewman Ian's burial, Captain Cobb wanted to lower the wine cellar beneath the sea again to cool the stored beer. Some of the crew wondered if Ian's body might somehow float into the cellar once it was submerged. They thought it might later frighten some unsuspecting visitor. Raleigh advised against it, saying it is bad luck, but Cobb insisted. He was in another one of his drinking moods. Once again, the ship flew low enough to submerge the wine cellar. What no one knew, Ian's body wasn't weighted down very well and floated up under the catwalk, only to get snagged on a dangling cable. Unaware to everyone, dark clouds began to form in the forward horizon. Soon the clouds were all around.

It was approximately three hours after Ian's burial. Cobb needed a cold beer. He ordered the ship raised enough to retrieve some casks of beer from the wine cellar. The ship slowly ascended, lifting the cellar and its walkways out of the water. Suddenly a valve jammed preventing the release of compressed gas into the balloon. The cellar walkway was now only a foot or two above the waves of what now had become a windy sea. As Cobb got down on the catwalk, he noticed the fins of several large sharks following the ship. Coming out of the cellar with a cask under each arm, he looked at the fins still following. Then suddenly, without warning, they all quickly veered off and were gone. After the casks were hauled up on the supply line, Cobb began to make his way up the rope ladder.

Something pulled at the rope ladder. No, it pulled at the ship. Cobb fell down on the catwalk. As he got back to his feet somewhat dazed, four tentacles from a giant squid rose out of the water on both sides of the ship. They seized the wine cellar and started trying to pull it under. Not wasting time, Cobb tried to get to the ladder, but a 5th tentacle rose up blocking his way, forcing him to back in the cellar. Lights were hung below the ship to see what was going on. Shocked by the sight below, several crewmen began firing their guns at the tentacles, but it seemed to have little effect. Seeing an opening, Cobb ran out and began to climb. About halfway up, a 6th tentacle came up and wrapped around his legs. All gunfire above was now focused at the tentacle holding the Captain. It finally relinquished its hold and Cobb started climbing again, but not before taking a stray bullet in his leg. At that point a lasso rope was thrown down. He grabbed onto it and was pulled up. Now the creature, with all eight tentacles wrapped around the wine cellar, began to pull it along with the rest of the ship down into what was now becoming a dark stormy sea. Raleigh gave the order to cut away the cellar. Crewmen began hacking away at the cellar lines with machetes. After several more gut-wrenching seconds the cellar and the giant squad finally gave way, falling into the sea. During the heat of battle, no one noticed the intense lightning in the distant horizon all around.

With the weight of the wine cellar gone, the ship began to ascend away from what was becoming a violent sea. A few minutes later they had ascended into the clouds, but not any closer to safety. The stormy clouds seemed to be closing in from all directions. The ship was beginning to spin in the violent winds. Both the stormy sea below and starlight above had disappeared. Then the clouds began to glow with a blue luminescence and started to swirl forming a tunnel. It was like a whirlpool on its side, and at the end of it was what looked like a cloud filled with intense lightening. Hermes was bobbing violently "Doorway! Doorway! "he shouted over and over.

"What is happening?" Raleigh asked.

"I don't know. I've never seen anything like it!" Cobb answered. Helpless against the wind, they were being blown toward the cloud of lightning. "Hang on!" Cobb shouted as it engulfed the ship. It was loud and violent. Cobb and Raleigh thought it was over. Under this stress, the ship would be torn apart in a matter of minutes, but the storm passed almost as quickly as it came. What was most unsettling was it was no longer night. They were in a thick gray fog of some kind. Judging by the color of light it felt like midday. Raleigh checked the altimeter; they were still ascending. Taken back by the light all around, Raleigh pulled out her pocket watch to check the time. According to it, the time was 9:30PM. The ship stopped its accent.

59. **WHEN A FIFTH TENTACLE** came up out of the sea Cobb was forced back to the wine cellar.

Cobb ordered everyone to check for any damage to the ship and any possible injuries to the crew. After learning there was only minor damage and no injuries, Raleigh ordered all who were not on duty to get some rest. Standing near the helm, Hermes began to bob back and forth again. "It's not safe here. There is a great disturbance below," he repeated over and over. As the ship continued to drift, it began to get dark. Night was coming. Cobb decided it was safer to stay at their current altitude until morning. During the night they could hear what sounded like occasional distant thunder. After what they had all been through, Cobb was having thoughts of returning home, but then he never found any of the exotic plants he was looking for. He knew he would have to try again at some point, in a place where there are no giant snakes or hostile natives.

At the first light, the ship was still enclosed in a thick fog. It was ascending so slowly that almost no one noticed. Breaking through the upper cloud tops, the Minerva came out into an area between cloud layers and was bathed in the early morning sun. After resting, Hermes returned to the helm. After a while he started bobbing again and speaking again, but this time he spoke so quietly that almost no one could hear him saying; "We should descend back into the clouds before it is too late." Raleigh looked at him without saying a word. There was a faint rumbling sound coming from below. Then suddenly with a horrifying clap of thunder, a rocket with wings blasted past the port side as it flew up in a near vertical climb. Everyone on deck was blown back by the concussion of air. Before anyone could react, a second rocket blasted by as it shot up past the port side. It was chasing the first one. As everyone watched, the second rocket started shooting at the first one, which had turned and was now diving back into the clouds. The pursuer followed, and in an instant, they were gone. "My God! What are they?" Cobb said as he got to his feet.

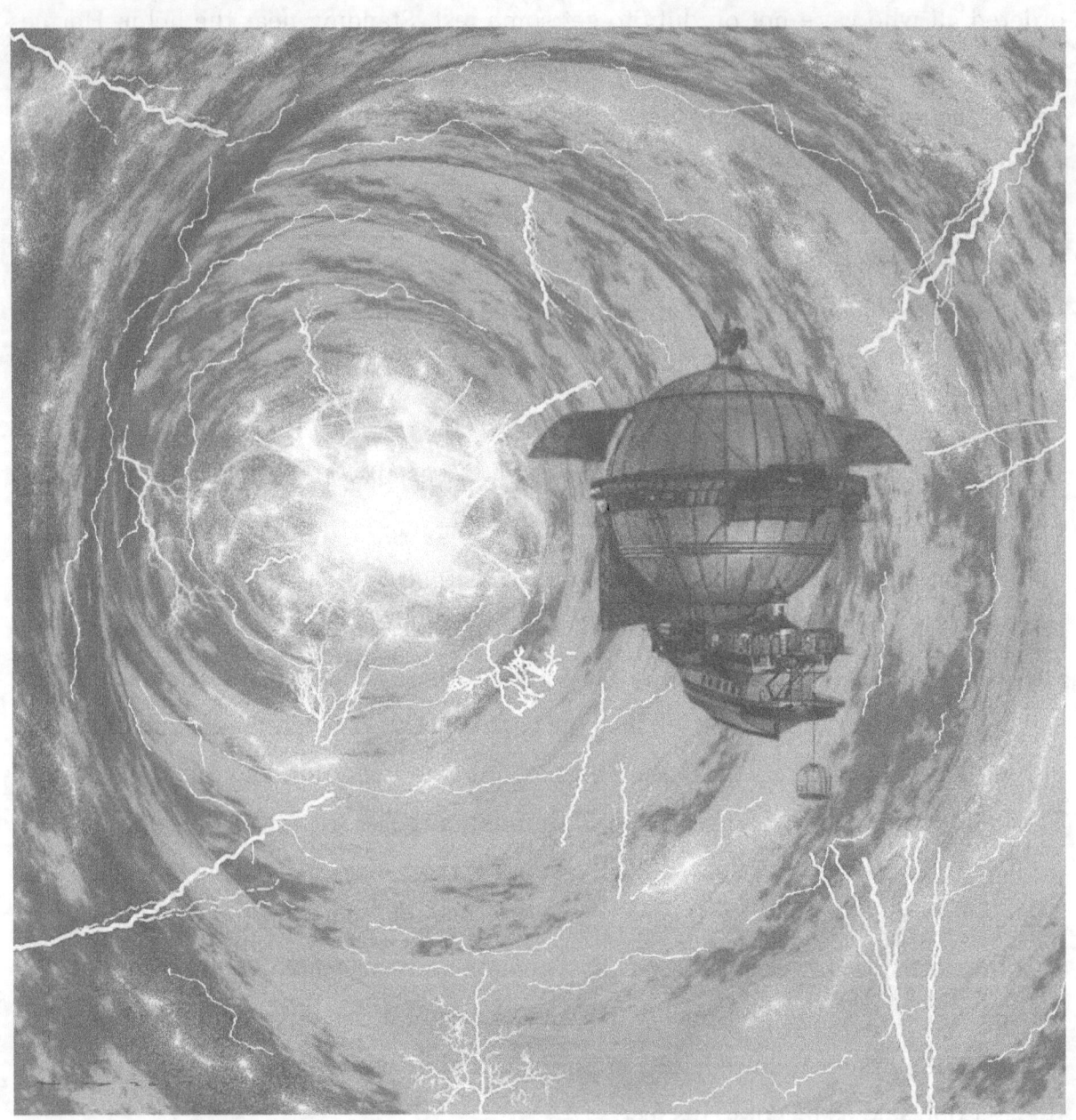

60. **THE MINERVA'S CREW** escaped from the sea monster below only to find themselves surrounded by blue glowing clouds filled with lightning.

"What do you think they are?" Raleigh asked.

"I don't know. If they decide to attack America we won't stand a chance," Cobb responded in a quiet voice, with his mouth hanging open.

For a while, all was calm again. After what just happened, Hadley was on the constant lookout with his telescope. "Captain, I see something far off the starboard side," he said as he handed his scope to Cobb. Cobb focused the scope to get a better look. Off in the distance there was another balloon ship, but this one was different. It was long like a cigar, and it was turning towards them. Looking at it through their telescopes, Cobb and Raleigh tried to make out what country it was from but couldn't tell. It was clearly another ship of advanced design. Later, Cobb described the ship in his log.

"As the ship got closer, I could see that it was more like a sealed, elongated, teardrop shaped balloon, turned on its side. At the front of the ship was a large crest of a yellow sun with eight points. At the narrow end, the rear of the ship, there were fins to control the ships direction. On each side of the ship there were small windmills that appeared to be turning fast enough to propel the ship forward. Above, on the top of the ship, was what appeared to be two pancake towers arranged in tandem and connected by an outdoor catwalk. Below the catwalk, on both sides of the ship, there were eight gun ports. The cannons appear to be the equivalent of 11 inch Dahlgren's. This was clearly a highly advanced war ship of some kind."

Cobb watched in amazement as the ship passed by on the starboard side. Some of Minerva's crew even waved at the crew on the other ship as it passed. They gave no response. They turned again and came along Minerva's port side. Cobb felt something was terribly wrong. Maybe they were curious about the Minerva as well. As they made a second close pass, their cannons opened fire, inflicting heavy damage. At least a third of the crew was killed instantly. Stunned by the horror, Cobb and his crew tried to react to what had just happened. When the Minerva departed Texas, it was thought to be the most advanced ship of its kind. No one imagined a battle taking place in the air. Cobb ordered all fires to be put out as fast as possible because the ship was venting gas. Raleigh led a detail to stop the leaks as fast as possible. If the hydrogen gas ignited that would be the end of the Minerva and its crew. It was only a miracle it didn't happen already.

61. **AS THE UNKNOWN SHIP MADE ANOTHER PASS** their cannons opened fire, inflecting heavy damage. At least a third of the crew was killed instantly.

With the loss of gas, they were descending into the lower cloud layer. As they descended, the faint sound of cannon fire below grew louder. Dropping below the clouds, they could see a great naval battle was in progress. Suddenly the ship that attacked them re-appeared not far away below the cloud layer. It started coming for another pass when aerial cannon fire from below struck its lower tail fin, causing it to break off its approach and ascend back into the thick clouds above. Using his telescope, Cobb got a good look that the ship that fired from below. It was flying an American flag. Raleigh's crew repaired the gas leaks, but the Minerva was still descending dangerously close to the battle below. It was only a matter of seconds before it would catch stray fire. Some parts of the gondola were still burning. Cobb ordered burning pieces cut loose if possible. To some degree it was working, but not enough to stop the ships descent. The next order was the hardest one he ever gave. He ordered all dead crewmen to be thrown off. It worked. The Minerva was rising away from danger. Once back up in the clouds, the ship was once again up in the thick haze. As they got higher, the sounds of the battle below grew fainter. Then the sounds of the enemy balloon ship could be heard. At first, they grew louder, than fainter as the two ships passed close in the thick fog, but not within sight of each other. From time to time the enemy would run silent. It was listening, hoping to find Cobb's ship. Cobb and Raleigh ordered everyone not to speak or make noise of any kind. After several more passes it went away, still searching.

The Minerva was still ascending slowly. The gray fog began to get lighter. No one heard the enemy ship coming back. As it approached, its downwind position concealed the sound from its engines. The enemy ship was above the cloud layer searching. No one knew the Minerva was directly below its path. Minerva's gas filled Rooster was the first part of the ship to rise up through the clouds directly in front of the approaching ship, which was moving too fast to avoid a collision. Its forward anchor got caught on the Rooster. Unable to slow or free itself, the enemy ship pitched forward. The gas in the Rooster ignited. The enemy ship's forward section caught fire. The Rooster was torn away from the Minerva just in time. Cobb and Raleigh watched in amazement as the burning enemy ship, unable to pull its nose up, plunged downward into the clouds. Moments later it crashed into the sea between the fighting ships below. Cobb was glad, "Well, it would seem that dammed Rooster actually had a purpose after all," he said quietly as he took a deep breath.

62. NO ONE KNEW the Minerva was rising up directly in the other ship's path. The forward anchor on the enemy ship got caught on Minerva's gas filled Rooster. Unable to slow or free itself, the ship pitched forward.

As they floated higher and higher away from the battle, Raleigh and Hadley did an assessment of the ship's damage. It was considerable. Everyone agreed it was too dangerous to continue the air voyage and would land the ship at the first place that was safe. Later, if the ship turned out to be damaged beyond repair, the surviving crew could return home by land or sea as the means became available. For the first time, Cobb realized his arm had been badly burned. He began to feel dizzy at the sight of it. As the crew began working to repair what remained of the ship, Raleigh patched Cobb's arm up in his cabin. When she was finished, Cobb looked out the window at the sunset over the cloud covered horizon. "You know, I thought the air voyage would be mostly calm like this," He was exhausted. Raleigh told him to rest up while she overlooked the repairs. Cobb passed out.

Later, Raleigh visited Hermes in his cabin. He was drawing sketches of what had just happened. Looking closer, Raleigh admired his work. As she looked around, she saw other drawings and sketches. It turned out he had been visually documenting the voyage. "These are very good. You're quite gifted. I just hope we will have a chance to share them with the folks back home," she said, looking at one of them.

"Not all of us will make it back. Another door in the clouds like the one we passed through is coming," he said, as he continued to sketch.

"What?" She asked.

"Another doorway is coming," he said.

Raleigh tried to ask him the details, but Hermes didn't answer. At this point in the voyage, they all knew Hermes had a tendency to simply stop communicating. She left his cabin.

63. **AS COBB AND HIS CREW WATCHED IN AMAZEMENT,** the burning enemy ship plunged downward into the clouds. Moments later it crashed into the sea between the fighting ships below.

64. MINERVA'S FIRST OFFICER: Dianna Raleigh.

24 hours later, Petrov and Thornton met with Lionheart in his quarters. "Captain, the good news is that we have been able to repair the fuses, but I can't guarantee they will be as reliable as before," Petrov said.

"Good work Petrov," Lionheart said.

"Captain, the fuses are not the real problem. When we came down the way we did, we used up nearly all of our reserve power. It takes a small flame to start a big fire."

"What are you saying Petrov?"

"We don't have the power to initialize start up, and unless we find a source, we are stuck here. Right now, we only have enough left to run the ship at current levels for another four days. After that we will be completely without power," Petrov said.

"Where can we go to get the kind power we will need in the early 17th century? If we can't find a source, we all better get used to herding goats, or whatever it is they do out here," Lionheart said, as he took a deep breath.

"Captain, I was thinking, if there is any truth to the legend Petrov was talking about earlier, there may be a suitable power source nearby for us to initiate startup, and also the possible location where Ms. West might have been taken to," Thornton said.

"Go on," Lionheart responded.

"I re-examined the telemetry sent back from our probe, more specifically, the moment the cameras started rolling shortly after it was fired from the ship. It turns out this lake is manmade. It is at the northern end of a very large canyon with many tributaries. Approximately 20 miles south of here, I saw something in one of the images I couldn't explain. It is not a natural feature. Here is an image of the area enlarged," Thornton said, as he laid it down on Lionheart's desk. The image showed several large vehicles going in and out of what looked like a false mountain face. On some of the vehicles there was what looked like a large iron cylinder with a pointed end.

As he leaned in closer, it was clear that Petrov was amazed by the image. "So, the legend is true. Captain, it was said that Count Vladislav had an underground city that had been built directly on the remains of an ancient settlement."

"Captain, as you can see, these are the land steamers like the one that likely left the tracks we saw earlier," Thornton continued, "I believe these cylinders they're carrying are actually the subterranean steamships, or the iron moles Petrov told us about. Sir, if the Russians developed a steam engine capable of driving these ships through solid earth, I believe they are... "

"...powered by some form of uranium steam engine?" Lionheart said, interrupting.

"Precisely! If these engines do exist, we have to find a way to possibly capture one and tap into its power source," Thornton said.

"Well done, Thornton. We will put together an away team to investigate. What is this to the south?" Lionheart asked pointing to an image that wasn't enlarged.

"It appears to be a rail line."

"Interesting," Lionheart said.

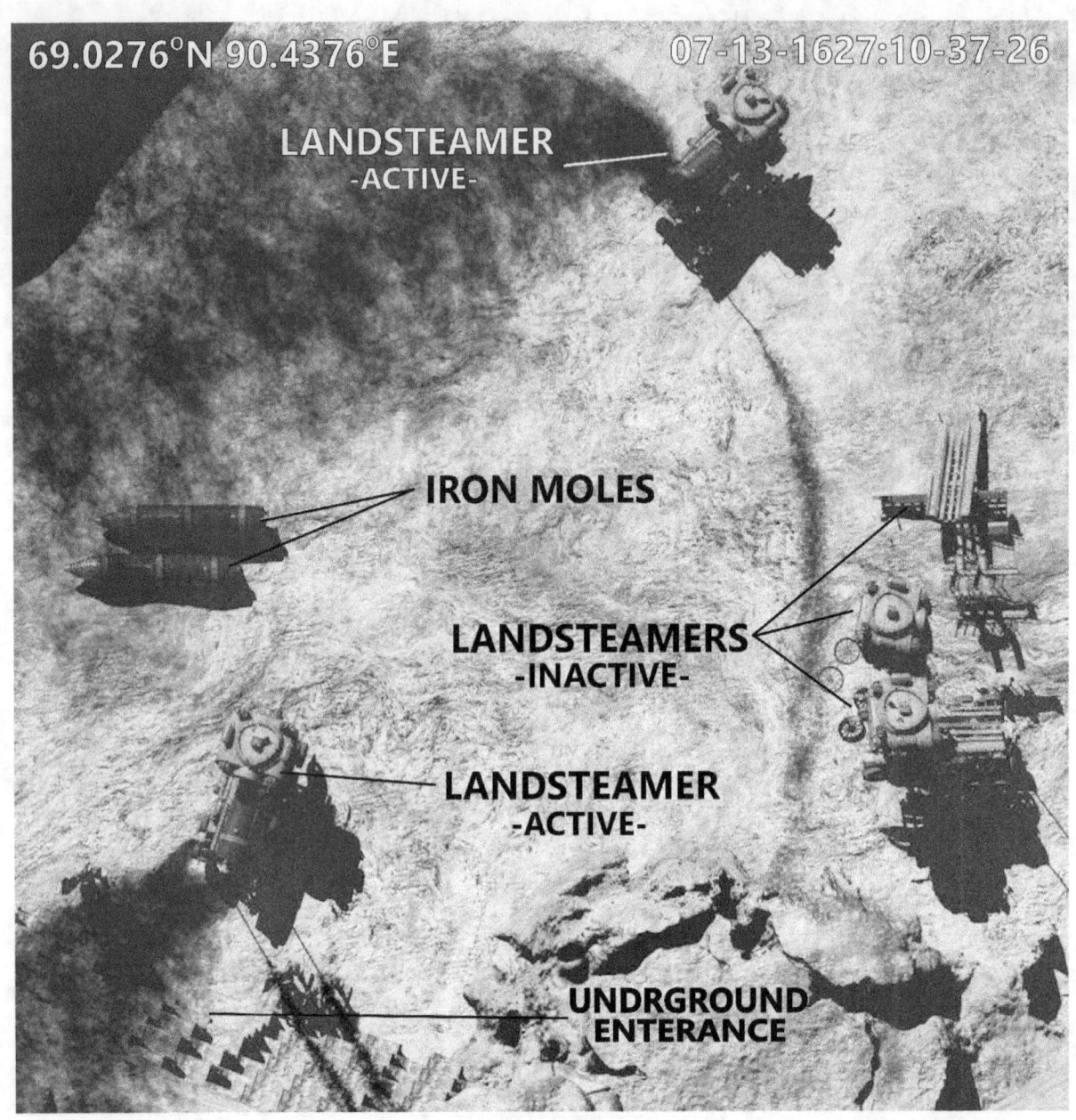

65. THORNTON'S TELEMETRY IMAGE of an area near the lake that shows unusual activity he couldn't fully explain.

Minerva had been drifting south for several hours. Raleigh wondered how much longer the ship could keep flying. At least they were away from the battle. There were no sounds of any kind except the gentle winds that carried the ship along. The clouds below began to break up as the late afternoon gave way to sunset. The Minerva was still over water, but where? A full moon was rising in the east. The orange clouds of sunset gave way to being moonlit with the fall of night. All was calm. Raleigh began to realize how exhausted she was. She retired to her cabin.

As the hours passed, a storm was forming on the horizon behind them. There were only distant silent flashes of lightning at first. The storm was approaching fast. Soon, the distant clap of thunder could be heard. Even though it was still distant, it was enough to cause Raleigh to return to the helm. Later Cobb awoke in his cabin to the violent shaking of the ship. The storm had caught up to them. Now there were bright flashes of lightening all around, and as before, the clouds all around were beginning to glow with a blue luminescence. Cobb made his way to the helm as fast as he could. "What is happening?!" he said, coming up behind Raleigh and Hadley.

"The lightning appeared a short time ago. I steered the ship to get clear of it, but it changed direction and started following us! There is no way to outrun it!" she said, struggling to control the helm.

"Oh my God!" Cobb said, as a blinding light engulfed the ship, rendering the crew unconscious. As before, the storm passed as quickly as it came. Once again, it was calm. Later, Cobb, Raleigh and the rest of the crew slowly began to open their eyes. As he came too, he looked around to see that everyone else had also been struck unconscious by the storm. This time, however, the storm seemed much more violent. As Cobb slowly got to his feet, he could see some of the others were waking up also. Both he and Hadley helped Raleigh as she was waking up.

"Where are we?" she asked as she got to her feet.

"Russia, we're over Russia," Hermes responded.

"How do you know?" Cobb asked. Hermes didn't answer. Instead, he turned and went back to his cabin.

"I guess that's all we are going to get out of him today," Hadley responded. It was late afternoon with scattered clouds. The land below was mostly covered in a rolling thick mist. From what they could see in the gaps of the mist, the landscape looked like green rolling tundra. "Well, wherever we are, it looks like we are definitely out in the middle of nowhere," Hadley said as he looked all around through his telescope.

"Captain, we no longer have the means to maintain altitude and are slowly descending. After passing through the last storm, we lost too much hydrogen, and the reserve tanks are almost empty. At our current altitude and rate of decent, I estimate we can only stay aloft for two hours," Marston said.

"All right. Very good. Marston, come with me. I think if we can remove some of the ships balloon superstructure, it might make the ship light enough to fly again. I knew when we lost that dammed Rooster back there, we also lost the lift it provided. Hadley, Raleigh, see if you can find a good place to land," Cobb said.

"Captain, Hermes is right. Look at this!" Hadley said, handing Cobb his telescope. Cobb focused the telescope at a lone wooden building off in the distance. It was a church, and the style of architecture was clearly Byzantine.

As Cobb and Marston made their way around the balloon superstructure, they could see that the rolling tundra below was becoming more rugged. The ship was coming down in a valley nestled between two large hills that were taller than the ship. "This is good. At least no one can see the ship from a distance here," Cobb thought. Raleigh landed the ship. As the thick rolling mist continued to slowly blow across the land, at times only the top of Minerva's balloon was visible. There was something about the mist that only Raleigh noticed, it was unusually warm. Generally, the air all around was cold, somewhere in the mid-forties, Fahrenheit, but the mist felt much warmer. It reminded Raleigh of the mist that rises from hot springs in the winter. The sky was turning orange with the setting sun. Cobb returned to the helm and found Raleigh waiting for him.

66. **AFTER THE STORM** subsided, it later became clear the Minerva was now somewhere over Russia.

"Captain, it's time. The remaining crew are assembled in what's left of the ships chapel," Raleigh said.

"Yes, of course. So much has happened. Until now we haven't even had time to mourn the loss of our crew. When nightfall comes, douse all outside lights. I don't want to run the risk of anyone spotting the ship," Cobb said, as they headed for the chapel.

As Cobb gave the burial service, he became painfully aware of the true condition of the crew. It seemed odd that there weren't any bodies to mourn over. Before the voyage he had several American and Texas flags stowed in his cabin in the unlikely event of crew fatalities. He honestly believed he would never have to use them. For a moment, he entertained the idea of abandoning the ship and making their way back on land. The idea was quickly put out of his head when he realized there were groups of people living in Russia's wilderness that no one would consider civilized. With that in mind, he knew unless he could get the ship to fly again, it was unlikely anyone would make it back.

Night had fallen. As a safety precaution, Cobb had the ship on black out. Windows were covered and no outside lights were burning. After the funeral service, several crew stepped out carrying lanterns. The rolling mist occasionally revealed the dark horizon all around. Before being told to put them out, something out in the dark horizon appeared. From that distance it first appeared as a green cloud that was constantly changing its form. It started moving toward the ship. It disappeared as another thick patch of mist rolled by in front of it. Once the horizon was clear again the green cloud was much closer. Everyone could see it wasn't a cloud at all, but rather a swarm of flying animals that had green glowing eyes. Before Cobb and Raleigh could order everyone back inside, the swarm was upon them. They flew past the lanterns so fast that no one could make out any of their features beyond their green glowing eyes and long tails.

After the first pass, everyone started running to take cover. Some of the crew managed to get below. The creatures made another pass. By this time most of the crew was either back inside the chapel or had taken cover below deck. Before they could get the chapel doors closed, one of creatures flew inside. As it flew around the ceiling, everyone could see it clearly now and became even more horrified. The creature had the body of a miniature lion, the wings of a bat, and a tail with a scorpion stinger. Everyone tried to shield themselves with hymnals as it darted down, trying to sting the crew with every pass. It came down at Cobb. He held up his Bible to block the stinger. The creature's stinger punctured the book and snatched it from his hands. It then flew off with the Bible stuck to its stinger. In the excitement, no one noticed the sound of gunfire outside. As the creature continued to fly around the ceiling, it did its best to shake the Bible off its tail.

After a few more lunges at the panicked crew, it finally freed its stinger. It made another dive at Cobb. This time he had no means to defend himself. As he raised his arm up to block, Raleigh jumped in front of him and took the sting in his place. At that moment, Marston and Hadley burst thru the chapel doors holding shotguns. As the creature circled above for another attack, they opened fire, killing the creature instantly. Having doused all light, the creature swarm outside circled the ship one more time, then flew off in the direction from where they first appeared.

Oblivious of everything, Cobb knelt down to attend Raleigh. She was starting to shake and become incoherent. Dr. Pike knelt down on the other side. "There is nothing I can do for her here. Captain, you and Hadley get her to her cabin. I'll meet you there with my bag." They lifted Raleigh off the floor. Later, in her cabin, Pike injected her with an antitoxin. "I don't even know if this will have any affect at all, but it may slow down the sting's poison," he said as he gave her the first injection.

67. HAVING STRUCK THE BIBLE with its stinger, the creature snatched it from Cobb's hands and continued to fly around the room.

"She seems to be stabilizing a little. I'm going to give her something to help her sleep. Two others have been stung also," Pike said.

"Who else was stung?" Cobb asked. "Crycheck and McMann," Pike said, as he got to his feet.

Hadley looked after Raleigh as she slept. Cobb and Pike stepped outside her cabin. "Doc, what do you think her chances are?"

"Not good. We don't even know what we are up against. It would be better if we knew more about these creatures," Pike said.

"Would an examination of the ones we shot help?"

"It would if we had one with its stinger still attached. All of the ones shot by Hadley and Marston had their stingers blown clean off. If I could get one intact, I might be able run some tests and find out what we are up against. These creatures, they seem familiar somehow, they remind me of something, but I can't place it, "Pike said.

"At first light I will lead a small heavily armed party off in the direction where they first appeared to see if we can find out where these creatures come from and, if possible, bring back an intact stinger by any means necessary," Cobb said.

"Do you think that is safe?"

"No, but I have the impression these creatures are nocturnal like bats and being attracted to light, they only attack at night. The swarm that attacked us last night didn't attack until we came out of the chapel. I believe it was the light from the chapel that attracted them. As an extra precaution, I'm going to have the barrels of our shotguns sawed off," Cobb said.

At first light, Cobb, Hadley along with crewmen Price, Randell, and McMillian, left the ship and headed off in the general direction where the creatures were first sighted. The rise from where they first appeared was approximately two miles from the ship. For the first time, Cobb and Hadley began to notice how much warmer the rolling mist was from the cold surrounding air. They also noticed it appeared to be coming from small openings in the rocky ground all around. "Those creatures could have come from any of these open fissures," Cobb said, as they came across one that was directly in front of them. "Well, I guess one is as good as the other," he said, as he stepped forward and began to step down.

It was a slow gradual decline. They could feel the warm air rising. Without lanterns, Cobb knew they couldn't go very far. Just as he was about to turn back, they could see a faint orange light below and began to hear distant sounds. Cobb was the first to notice it. The sounds were not natural, they were manmade, like the sounds of a busy shipyard. It was too dark to see their immediate surroundings. With only the faint light below to guide them, they stumbled along. As they descended, the air was getting hotter, and the industrial sounds got louder. Among the sounds of hissing steam and machinery, they also began to hear a faint snap or cracking sound. As they reached the lower end of the tunnel, they crouched down low so not to be seen. Moving slowly, Cobb and his men made their way out on to a ledge. They found themselves at the mouth of a ceiling air vent that overlooked a vast cavern. Being somewhat overwhelmed by its size, Cobb didn't realize at first that his mouth was hanging open.

The cavern looked to be several hundred feet across. Below was a vast industrial complex that was processing molten ore. The hot steamy air, orange glow and smell of molten ore, gave Cobb the impression that they had accidentally stumbled onto a nest of iron dragons. The complex was like a scene from Dante's inferno. It was difficult to see it clearly through all the rising steam. Everyone was amazed by the scale of the project. As Hadley looked around, he could see that the heat from this underground complex was clearly the source of the warm misty air above. Judging by the vast area above covered by the manmade mist, he determined that the size of the complex itself must be very large, possibly extending for great distances in all directions. It was large enough to be considered an underground city.

As Cobb and his party looked closer at the activity below, they could see peasant slaves being forced to push ore cars. The cracking sounds came from task masters cracking their whips over them. "So, I see slavery is alive and well in Russia," Cobb said quietly. It was clear to him that if they were captured, they would most likely be killed directly or die in slavery. The ledge they were on continued in both directions into other caverns.

68. COBB AND HIS PARTY found themselves at the mouth of a ceiling air vent that overlooked a vast cavern. The complex was like a scene from Dante's inferno.

"I never expected to find anything like this," Hadley said.

"Yes, given the number of open fissures we saw above, those creatures could have come from anywhere. With all of this, I'm surprised there are no more guards around. "We can't go any further from here," Cobb said.

"It's unlikely that they need any outside security. This place is truly out in the middle of nowhere. I don't think anyone even knows it is here. If a slave escaped, there are only hundreds of miles of cold wilderness in all directions..."Hadley said. "...and if you didn't die from starvation and exposure, a swarm of those creatures would find you," Cobb said, as they all quietly withdrew back into the tunnel and returned to the ship.

Shipeda Saudee

After a long trek in their amphibian, Lionheart's party was almost at the location where the probe sighted the land steamers. The area was just beyond the edge of the cliff up ahead. Lionheart decided it would be best to approach on foot to avoid being seen. Slowly moving in a crouched position, Lionheart, Thornton and Petrov made their way to the edge of the cliff. As they got closer, they could hear the sounds of people and machinery in the canyon below. Looking down, they were all amazed at the activity taking place in such a remote part of the world. The activity in the rocky valley below was like a busy harbor, except this was on land. The valley was surrounded on three sides by towering cliffs that were far too steep to climb. It was like a tributary that opened out to an area of vast rolling planes to the east. The grand rock face where the valley ended was almost unnoticeable because of the four massive stone gargoyle figures that flanked what looked like the entrance to an underground city. The stone figures were badly worn from enduring many centuries of exposure to the sun and weather. Lionheart wondered if it was built as far back as ancient Mesopotamia. As they watched, a land steamer was coming out and another was going in.

"So that is the false mountain side we saw in the images," Lionheart said.

"Shipeda Saudee," Petrov said quietly to himself.

"What?" Thornton asked.

"According to the legend of the Siberian Kings, the settlement actually consisted of smaller settlements. Shipeda Saudee was said to be the harbor for the ships that sailed beneath the Earth. They were called iron moles. Apparently, the legend it true. Until now I never would have believed it," Petrov said.

Lionheart decided to follow the outbound land steamer from a safe distance. It led them to an area approximately 25 miles [40.2k] away. It wasn't until then that everyone noticed for the first time that the air was very cold and there were patches of snow and ice all around. Back near the Onyx Tower, the misty air was much warmer. This was also true for the surrounding land. Now that they were outside the area, the air was clear and cold. Thornton pointed out it was due to the fact that warm air was constantly rising out of small open fissures all around the lake and canyon area.

69. LIONHEART'S PARTY discovers Shipeda Saudee. As grand as it was, Lionheart couldn't stop thinking about West. He believed West had been taken underground somewhere. It was the only thing that would explain why no location signal had been received from the transmitter installed in West.

As they watched from a safe distance, the giant Russian land steamer came to a stop. Several men came out of the steamer's pilot house and boarded the iron mole. Soon after, the sound of a second engine could be heard. This engine was powerful. So much so that Lionheart and the others could feel the ground vibration from it. The nose of the iron mole had counter rotating rings that started to spin. The cradle that the iron mole was resting on, slowly began to tilt downward. Now pointing down toward the Earth, the iron mole slowly began to move forward. The moment its nose made ground contact, the ship started digging, spewing a cloud of dirt and rocks in all directions. Like a train slowly moving into a tunnel, the iron ship burrowed into the Earth. Moments later, it was gone, leaving only a small mountain of dirt and rubble behind that sealed the hole it entered. The ground vibration dissipated a few minutes later. Lionheart became curious.

"If the iron mole doesn't leave a clear tunnel behind when it digs, what was its purpose?" he wondered.

Having launched the iron mole, the land steamer slowly backed away from the small manmade mountain it left behind and razed its cradle back to a horizontal position.

"Well Thornton, I see your point. Any ship that has the power necessary to submerge into solid ground like what we just witnessed must have a very strong power source, more than enough for our needs. Still, how is it possible the Russians could have developed an engine with that kind of power back in 1627? The only type of engine it could possibly be is a uranium steam engine, and it won't be invented until many years from now," Lionheart said.

"I wonder if we are not the first ship from the future to come to this place and time. Captain, if my guess is correct that subterranean steamship, or iron mole, can't stay submerged for long. It's also my guess, that land steamer is headed for a retrieval point somewhere not far away," Thornton said.

"Why would you say that?" Lionheart asked.

"It's because any kind of vessel that has enough power to dig its way through solid rock has to be creating an enormous amount of heat, and they have no way of dissipating it. If they stay under too long the crew will..." Thornton said. "...I think the expression is 'become toast'," Petrov said, interrupting.

"I think we should follow the land steamer and see where it goes," Thornton said.

70. AS LIONHEART'S TEAM WATCHED from a safe distance, the Russian land steamer launched an iron mole into the Earth.

Lionheart was also curious. The land steamer made its way to a nearby dry river valley to the north. Once there, it stopped. The rocky terrain nearby made it possible for Lionheart's party to get close without being seen. The land steamer didn't have to wait long. Lionheart and the others began to feel a vibration in the ground. A moment later the iron mole came out of the hillside. Once it was completely above ground, it came to rest, with its engines shutting down not far from the land steamer. Hatches opened and its crew got out. As they emerged, they stepped away from the vehicle. It was hard to tell from a distance, but the crew looked hot and exhausted as they emerged from the thick steamy air rising out of the hatches. Many of them got down on one knee and tried to cool down by fanning themselves. A group of men came from the land steamer and secured heavy cables to the iron mole. It was then hauled back up onto the land steamer's cradle. After the iron mole was loaded up and the both crews were back on board, the land steamer slowly headed back toward Shipeda Saudee.

"We need to find out more. Somehow, we need to get into one of those iron moles before we can devise a plan," Lionheart said quietly.

"Look!" Thornton said, pointing to the departing land steamer. "Someone jumped down from the steamers under frame and ran into the rocks!"

Lionheart lifted his telescope to get a better look. "Well, whoever he is, I don't think anyone saw him jump. No one is coming after him." Lionheart waited for a short time until the land steamer was further away.

"It looks like a technician who is trying to escape," Petrov said, looking through his telescope.

"He may know something that could help us. Let's pick him up," Lionheart said, as he retracted his scope.

Lionheart's party didn't have to travel very far before they came upon him. The man was crawling on the ground as he tried to get away. Speaking in Russian, Petrov tried to reassure him they meant no harm. His leg was bleeding and he passed out from the pain shortly after Lionheart's party reached him.

71. LIONHEART'S PARTY caught up to the Russian technician that had escaped from the land steamer. His leg was hurt. Petrov tried to assure him that they met no harm. He identified himself as Ivanov.

"He is hurt pretty bad Captain," Thornton said.

"Let's get him back to the ship," Lionheart said.

As Lionheart's party headed back to the lake, they took a different route and came upon another hidden valley. Down in the middle of it was the Minerva. Lionheart recognized it immediately from his history.

"That ship over there is the Minerva. It sailed from Texas in the mid 1500's. What the hell is it doing here?" Lionheart quietly asked himself.

"It's possible the same anomaly that brought us here might have also brought the Minerva as well," Thornton said.

"I don't know. The hull looks badly damaged. It looks like it was hit from cannon fire." Lionheart said looking through his telescope.

"We need to get back to the tower. Ivanov needs medical attention." Thornton said as they both quietly backed away from the cliff.

Later, back at the Onyx tower, Lionheart couldn't stop thinking about the Minerva. He wondered what it was doing here. He also remembered Margret Dana's early experiments in inter-dimensional physics when she first tried to create doorways that connected places that were far apart. He recalled some of her journals told of unintentional doorways opening under certain circumstances. In fact, one time while attempting to create a doorway (or anomaly) between California and Southern England, a third doorway opened to Russia and one of those deadly flying creatures flew into Dana's lab. Lionheart wondered if both the Onyx Tower and the Minerva were brought through another anomaly that had three doorways. Who was the anomaly intended for, and who was controlling it? Considering the fact that his ship had been sabotaged and Ms. West was missing, Lionheart assumed the portal must have been intended for him. He also wondered again about Dana's other backer, the mysterious Dr. Serco, an industry leader that no one knew much about.

72. ON THEIR RETURN TO THE TOWER Lionheart and Thornton came upon the Minerva balloon ship. The hull looked badly damaged from battle and the crew was in the process of making repairs.

As Lionheart sat in his cabin, he continued to wonder what the best course of action would be. His thoughts were interrupted when Thornton knocked and came in.

"Captain, the man we picked up has regained consciousness and is in sick bay with Connors and Petrov," Thornton said. Moments later, Lionheart was down in sick bay.

"How is our patient? I was told he was awake," Lionheart asked in a quiet voice, as he came up behind Connors.

"He was until a few minutes ago. After Petrov spoke to him, he fell back asleep."

"Is he going to be, OK? What was his condition?" Lionheart asked.

"Well, he doesn't have a broken leg like everyone thought. It's a prosthetic below the knee. He must have fallen hard when he jumped out of that land steamer because that solid oak false leg of his was cracked right down the middle. That is what caused his knee to bleed so badly. The pain must have been overwhelming," Connors said.

"Petrov, have you found out anything?"

"Yes Captain, I spoke with him at length. He is Alexi Ivanov, an engineering technician that helped Count Vladislav develop the subterranean steamships we saw earlier," Petrov said.

"Count Vladislav?" Lionheart asked.

"Yes, according to Ivanov, the chief administrators of the settlement here are Count Vladislav and another who is known only as Krnobov. The Count is a direct relation to Czar Alexander. Although the way Ivanov spoke of him, I have the impression the Count is a member of the royal family that no one wants to associate with. Very little is known about Krnobov. It is rumored he descends from aristocracy."

"Did Ivanov say anything about what goes on out here?"

"Oh yes. This settlement is actually a very large mining operation, and according to Ivanov, it may be the largest in the world. Apparently, the Count has an agreement with the Czar. As long as the ore flows to Moscow in the west, he is allowed to run his little empire out here as he sees fit." Petrov said, as he paused for a moment.

"Did he say why he jumped off the land steamer? Was he trying to escape?" Lionheart asked.

"Yes, he was trying to make it to a rail line that is just to the south of here to ride one of the ore trains back to Moscow. Ivanov was also carrying several maps, diagrams, drawings, and photographs as proof of what was going on out here," Petrov said. In fact, he said one train is leaving tonight and Captain, a mechanical person they recovered is going to be on it," Petrov said.

"We have to intercept that train. How does he know about West?" Lionheart asked.

"Ivanov said one of the patrols scouting the lake shore came upon two dead men and a mechanical person. They left the bodies, but the mechanical person was brought back and taken to engineering for examination. He said when they were unable to turn it back on, the Count wanted it sent to Moscow. Ms. West will be in the only cargo van on the ore train." Petrov said.

"We need to have another look at the aerial images our probe sent back of that rail line, and I want to have a look at the maps Ivanov was carrying. I think our ship's cartographer McRandel might also be interested in seeing them." Lionheart said.

The Train

For 10 years he wondered how long it would last. While the last three cars, the cars of death, were brought up and hitched to the back of the train, the engineer slowly climbed up into the locomotive. Every time he departed from the underground city of Antopav, he wondered if anyone would ever find out about the death train. The first 10 cars were filled with ore. The 11th was a cargo van. And the last three were filled with dead bodies. Both Vladislav and Krnobov felt that having the death cars at the very back of the train was a sufficient distance to keep the stench from overwhelming the train crew.

The first stop would be at an old open strip mine just over a hundred miles [161 kilometers] away. Not long after they began dumping bodies there, it became known as the Valley Of Bones. Once the train arrived there, the last three cars would be unhitched, and the train would continue on to Moscow. "There had to be hundreds of thousands by now," the engineer thought, as the train slowly pulled away. Most of them were serfs from local villages, and a few were skilled labor. All of them had one thing in common, they were abducted and forced to work here against their will.

Under the cover of darkness, the train from Antopav made its way into the cold surrounding wilderness. Soon the train would be alone with no civilization in any direction for miles as it followed the winding track through the rolling tundra. They would reach the Valley Of Bones in three hours. There was something up ahead. The engineer could see that a large boulder had rolled down a hill and landed over one of the rails. It looked small enough not to damage the rail, but large enough to possibly derail the train. Not wasting any time, the engineer was able to stop the train just 20 feet [6 meters] from the boulder. He got out with the fireman and rolled the boulder off the rail. The rail was undamaged, just as he thought. There was a strange, sweet smell in the air. At first, he thought it might be a plant blooming nearby. He started to feel disoriented. Looking down he took a deep breath. Looking over at the fireman he could see that he was also having the same problem.

73. **THE TRAIN DEPARTD FROM** the underground city of Antopav

The next thing the train engineer and fireman knew they were both getting up off the ground as they regained consciousness. Whatever it was it seemed to pass as quickly as it came. They both dusted themselves off and climbed back into the locomotive. The fireman was surprised to see the engines fire had burned way down. It needed to be stoked quickly to maintain the boiler temperature. The boiler's temp and pressure

144

gauges indicated a loss. Both of them wondered how it could have fallen so quickly, as they were only out for a short time. The engineer looked at his watch. He was surprised to see that nearly a half hour had passed. The fireman's watch showed the same thing. The engineer stepped out to look over the train while the fireman stoked the fire. There was no sign of anything being wrong. The sweet smell that was in the air was gone. He climbed back into the engine, and they continued on their journey.

Lionheart's rescue plan was confirmed when they received the locator signal from West when the train emerged from the underground. They knew once the train had stopped and the crew was rendered unconscious, it would be a simple matter to locate and retrieve West. Once West was off the train, the crate she was in was resealed and placed back where it was. West had been very clever. She pretended to deactivate herself while in captivity but was recording everything around her at the same time. She also gave a high voltage shock when anyone tried to tamper with her. That is why they decided to send her to Moscow. As the rescue party headed back in the amphibian, Lionheart looked back at Ms. West. Except for some scratches on the back of her head, she looked completely undamaged. He wanted to get her back to the ship as soon as possible to make sure she wasn't damaged or had been tampered with. He also wanted to see if she could provide any clues as to why Andrews and Johnson would go on a suicide mission to crash the ship and everyone in it. Lionheart was relieved that the plan the stop the train and rescue Ms. West went so smoothly.

Later in Petrov's lab, Ms. West was fully examined and released. Lionheart was relieved to hear her voice again. West said very little. Lionheart felt West was analyzing everything that happened before speaking at length. She had no reaction after being updated on the ships status and everything that happened during her absence. She simply asked to resume her duties and return to the library.

"Ms. West," Lionheart said, as she was about to leave the room, "I'm very relieved to have you back on board," West nodded at his comment then left the room.

As Lionheart sat alone in his cabin, he wondered if he and his crew would be trapped back in the year 1627. What would they do? Where would they go? In a worst case, the

Onyx Tower would have to be destroyed to prevent disrupting the future. There was a knock at the door. It was Connors.

"I have to hand it to you Doctor. Your plan worked perfectly. The Tama gas completely subdued the train crew, and we were able to recover Ms. West without any problem. The Russians were not alerted to our presence and most importantly, no harm came to anyone. I just poured myself a drink. Would you care to join me?" Lionheart said, as the Doctor entered.

"Yes. I could use one. The crew knows our power is only going to last so long and everyone is starting to get edgy," Connors said, as she sat down.

There was another knock at his door. This time it was Thornton.

"Captain, I think I know how we are going to get out of here or perhaps the general direction we are going to take," Thornton said, as he entered Lionheart's cabin. "Ms. West became extremely interested about the Minerva when she heard we encountered it and looked to see if there was any history related to it. According to Minerva's history, the ship departed on its maiden voyage in May 1555. Approximately six weeks later, it crashed off the coast of Honduras with the few remaining members of its crew. According to official accounts of the crew, they only encountered heavy storms over South America. There was nothing unusual reported. Whatever happens- the Minerva is going to make it back, "Thornton said.

"I don't suppose Ms. West found anything about us?" Lionheart asked.

"Not directly. But one of Minerva's surviving crew members was a boy, Hermes Butchart. He was said to be autistic, but in spite of that, he was an excellent illustrator. Not long after he returned home, an illustrated children's book was published by his mother. It was called *Children of the Balloon*. After Ms. West showed the file to me, she printed a quote from the end of the story. *"The tower children restored the queen of the air. To give thanks, the children of the balloon helped the children of the tower return to their kingdom in the clouds..."* Thornton sat the open page down in front of Lionheart. The illustration showed the late sun beaming through the clouds. The Minerva was close by and off in the distance, not too far away was a Tower ascending into the clouds. As Lionheart leaned in to get a closer look, he could see the Tower was clearly his ship, the Onyx Tower.

"That is definitely the Onyx Tower," Lionheart said. "So, according to this, we will make it out of here. If this children's book is part of our history, we have to make contact with Minerva's crew."

74. LIONHEART LEARNS THE future of the Onyx Tower and the Minerva through a historic children's book Thorton had refabricated from the ships library.

The Old Church

At first light Cobb, Hadley, along with crewmen Price, Randell and McMillian, set off on yet another expedition to find out where the creatures came from. Before leaving the ship, Hermes approached Cobb saying "Captain, where you find great good, you also find great evil". Then in his usual manner, he turned and went back to his cabin. Raleigh was getting worse. They knew they didn't have much time left to save her. Even if a creature was found intact, Dr. Pike wasn't sure he could work out an antidote in time. Cobb's search party had already made several attempts to find the underground source of the creatures, but so far, they had only discovered cave openings that led to parts of the vast mining complex below.

Once again Cobb's party headed off in the general direction where the creatures first appeared. After reaching the first rise they stopped to rest. They could see the old wooden church they spotted days earlier, before landing. It stood alone in the distant horizon. There was a faint mist all around it. Cobb and the others wondered how a church that grand could even exist out in the middle of nowhere. He believed it must be the only remaining part of a settlement that was plundered, and its people became part of the slave force working below. Cobb began to think about what Hermes said just before leaving the ship.

"If anyone lived here, there is no trace of them now," Hadley said.

"Judging by the size of the church, there must have been a large village at the very least. Where could they have all gone? Aside from the church, there is absolutely nothing else around that I can see. Let's investigate. It's the one place we haven't looked," Cobb said. The wooden church was a very tall building. As they approached the entrance, Cobb was amazed at its size. Its doors were slightly open. There was a warm mist coming out, and it was dark inside. They drew their guns before entering and were surprised how much warmer it was inside. As expected, the interior was cavernous. As they looked around the interior, they could see most of the pews had been broken up and scattered all around the floor. Fearing that they might stir the creatures, Cobb and the others moved very quietly.

"Stop!" Hadley said in a quiet voice.

"What is it Hadley?" Cobb asked.

"It's the silence. There are no birds. There are always birds in abandoned buildings like this," Hadley said.

"I can hear a faint breeze, but it isn't coming from the outside. It sounds like it is coming from over there," Price said, as he pointed at the altar. There were occasional puffs of misty air coming up from behind it. The sight of it had a general ghostly effect. With each misty puff it was like a soul was rising up from the altar. Behind the altar there was a large opening through the broken wooden floor. It turned out to be the entrance of a small sloping cave leading underground. At first, it looked as though the old broken off boards had simply rotted away. Hadley knelt down to have a closer look. Many of the pieces had scratches on the underside. They all had the impression the opening might have been created by the creatures trying to claw their way out.

As they all leaned over to get a closer look, they could feel the warm moist air rising from below. "You would think after all the times we have gone underground, we would have brought lanterns." Hadley said.

Cobb stepped back and looked around. He found an old ceremonial cloth on the altar and tore it in half. He then wrapped it around a broken dowel from one of the pews and set fire to it.

"Captain, aren't you afraid that might attract the creatures?" McMillian asked.

"I'm going to step down a ways to see if I can see anything," Cobb said, as he descended into the opening. The tunnel was at an angle that allowed Cobb to walk almost upright. As he stepped further, the torch flame flickered in the wind coming from below. Cobb knew the tunnel was definitely part of a much larger underground passage. He wasn't sure, but for a moment he thought he saw a faint glowing light ahead. It was so faint he knew to see more clearly, he would have to put his torch out. Cobb stopped, turned, and told Hadley to hand the torch back to Price, the last man in line.

"Captain, what is it? What do you see? "Hadley asked.

"I'm not sure," Cobb replied. Cobb looked ahead. This time he could see the faint orange glow up ahead more clearly. There was something there. It wasn't just his imagination. "McMillan, I want you Randell, and Price to stay here. Hadley and I are going on up ahead to see what the source of that light is," Cobb said.

Cobb and Hadley stumbled along as they left the group behind them. The orange glow got brighter and brighter until they could clearly see that it was caused by torch lights in a cavern ahead. Moving slowly and quietly they approached the entrance to the cavern. It had a large oval area with a slightly sloping rocky floor. Cobb and Hadley were at the lower end of it. The light they saw came from two large lanterns suspended from ground poles at the far end of the cavern. Unlike other caves they had explored, the humidity here had gone up considerably. For the first time, Cobb began to feel uncomfortable in his heavy clothes. On the opposite wall at the far end of the cavern was a glass wall that stretched all the way to the cavern ceiling. Even though the cavern was lit, it was still very dark.

Coming out of the shadows, Cobb and Hadley made their way out into the cavern center. It was still too dark to see the ground clearly. As they walked, the ground they walked on began to crunch beneath their feet. As they got closer to the dimly lit lanterns, two wooden life size crosses nearby became clearly visible.

"Captain, I have a bad feeling about this. Let's get out of here," Hadley said. Cobb turned around to look back as Hadley motioned for him to look down. All around them were human skeletons that covered the entire cavern floor. There was nowhere to step without crunching their bones. A cold chill came over Cobb as he looked around. "There has to be hundreds of them," he said quietly.

"What do you suppose that is over there?" Cobb asked as he pointed to the glass wall. The wall was lit up from the far side. It was almost bright enough to be daylight. Cobb stepped closer. As he got closer, he could see that the glass had so much condensation on the far side that it almost made it translucent, but not transparent. "I think we should leave here now," Hadley said.

75. **AS COBB AND HADLEY WALKED,** they soon realized the floor of the cave was covered with human bones.

"We will. I just want to get a better look," Cobb said, as he got closer to the glass. He couldn't make it out, but there appeared to be shadows of large green, twisting vines on the far side. It gave Cobb the impression of a jungle setting. As Cobb got right up against the glass, he could just make out the moving shadows of flying creatures like those that attacked when they first arrived. He could just see the green glowing eyes of the ones that were close to the wall where he was. Suddenly one of the creatures hit the glass where he was standing. Cobb quickly lunged back in fear. Hadley's heart was pounding.

After the creature struck the glass, Cobb was afraid to get too close to the wall. As he stepped back, he became aware that there were two large metal doors in the glass wall not far from where he was standing. Cobb could see the doors only opened from the far side. There was no way to enter. One led into the jungle. The other led not to the jungle on the far side, but rather to a glass tunnel that passed through it.

"What the hell is all this? It looks like we have stumbled into some kind of animal breeding farm," Cobb said, with wonder, as he looked all around the wall.

"Yes. That is probably what it is. Can we get out of here now?" Hadley asked.

"OK, quick-, I can hear someone coming!" Cobb said, as he and Hadley hurried back to the connecting tunnel entrance.

As they watched from the darkness, they could see shadow figures approaching one of the doors from the far side. The door slid open with a deep heavy sound. Cobb wondered if they were made of iron. Five men came out. Two men were in chains and one limped along as best he could to stay ahead of the two guards prodding them from behind. The guards chained them to separate crosses. Once the prisoners were secured, the guards said something to them in Russian. Cobb and Hadley couldn't understand what the leader was saying. When he was finished, the leader and the two guards stepped back through the door closing it behind them.

76. AS THEY EXPLORED THE CAVERN beneath the old, abandoned church, Cobb and Hadley discovered what appeared to be an underground greenhouse for breeding the creatures that attacked the Minerva.

Hadley started to move toward the prisoners when Cobb suddenly grabbed his arm stopping him. "Where are you going?" he asked.

"I'm going to get a closer look at the prisoners, I have a feeling they are not criminals," Hadley said.

Cobb grabbed Hadley's arm again. This time it was because they could hear the sound of the other door opening. This was the second door that led directly into the creature infested greenhouse.

"Cobb, cover me!" Hadley said as he ran toward the first prisoner. Cobb ran over and tried to close the door, but after it wouldn't budge, he stepped back and aimed his gun into the open doorway. Hadley began trying to free the prisoner but wasn't having much luck. As Cobb watched he could see the green glowing eyes moving just inside the thick fog coming out of the greenhouse chamber.

"Hadley, we don't have much time!" Cobb said, as he raised his gun to fire.

Hadley motioned at the prisoner to get down low, as he pulled a pistol from his belt and fired a round at each of his ankle chains. Responding to the sound of gunfire, several creatures came out of the fog towards the door. Cobb fired his gun twice. It was enough, but more were coming. Hadley freed the second prisoner. As they all ran back to the entrance of the dark cavern, the second prisoner began to stumble as he fell behind. Hadley turned back to help him up. With his gun still aimed back at the open doorway to the greenhouse, Cobb tried to run backwards as fast as he could. As he reached the passageway, he saw the green glowing eyes of the creatures as they flew into the room. "Tiesposka!" the second prisoner said as he tried to get back up. Before he could do so, the creatures were upon him. There was nothing anyone could do. Cobb fired into the creatures that had swarmed down on the second prisoner. Not wasting any time, Hadley and the first prisoner began to make their way back up the tunnel. Cobb stayed behind to cover them as best he could. As he watched, the creatures began to fly around the cavern. As they did so, they were joined by a larger swarm that flew in from the greenhouse. Even though the second prisoner was already dead the creatures continued to sting him repeatedly. Cobb watched in horror as they quickly reduced the prisoner to a skeleton after stinging him. His bones were pushed in all directions as the creatures continued to fight over any scrap of remaining flesh.

"Christ-All-Mighty!" Cobb said quietly as he stepped back. As he did so, there was a loud crunch of bones that alerted the creatures to his presence. In an instant, they took flight in pursuit of their next meal. A cold chill came over Cobb as all those glowing eyes came toward him like a green cloud of death.

"Run!" Cobb yelled out as he started back up the passageway behind Hadley and the first prisoner. With death not far behind, they got up as fast as they could while still stumbling over rocks in the darkness. Looking up, they could see the torches of the other members of their party. As Cobb got closer, he continued to yell at the others to keep running. Seconds later the three got up to where the others had waited. Cobb glanced behind him. He could see the swirling cloud-like glow caused by the creature's eyes as they flew up the tunnel from behind. Cobb reasoned if they could get out in time to close the church doors, it might be enough to contain them, but the creatures were closing fast.

Cobb stopped, turned back, and started firing back into the tunnel. It suddenly occurred to him, with the creatures confined in the tunnel, he was likely to kill more of them. Hadley stopped and started firing his gun. The prisoner kept trying to make his way up. With Cobb and Hadley firing down on them, the creatures were no longer advancing. They both kept firing until they ran out of shells. During the shooting, Cobb and Hadley could see a lot of glowing eyes flickering off as the creatures were being killed off, but more new glowing eyes were appearing. The swarm appeared to be renewing itself as more creatures entered the tunnel. They started advancing again. Cobb and Hadley dropped their guns and began running. As they got back up into the church, McMillan and the others pulled them out, and then began shooting their guns back down at the approaching creatures.

"Help me with this altar!" Cobb said as he, Hadley and the others tried to push it over to block the cave entrance. The creatures began to fly out through the openings around the altar. Cobb and the others ran out of the chapel. They knew they couldn't turn and close the doors in time to stop the creatures. Cobb knew it was the end. He knew the creatures would catch up to them on open ground. Then it would be over. They ran out, away from the church as fast as they could, not looking back. Suddenly there was a loud clap of thunder. Then another, followed by another. Cobb and his party dove to the ground face down.

There was silence. Cobb slowly looked up. There was no sign of the creatures on either side of them. As he and the others slowly got to their feet they turned around. The ground was littered with the burned, smoking bodies of creatures everywhere behind them. Standing just outside area of dead creatures were several men. Three of them were holding what looked like large rifle guns that had barrels made of a glowing crystal material. As Cobb looked back at the men, it was clear that one of them was the leader. He slowly stepped toward Cobb saying "Captain Cobb I presume. I have heard of you. I'm Captain Lionheart, and I'm very glad to make your acquaintance," Lionheart said, as he extended his hand to help Cobb up.

Cobb was stunned. He held his hand out to shake Lionheart's hand with his mouth hanging open.

"Do I know you? How do you know who I am?" Cobb asked as he got to his feet.

"We have never met, but I have read about you and your ship, the Minerva. Your story was in all the newspapers," Lionheart said.

"Of course, I forget about that. I just didn't expect to run into anyone who would know about us here. You speak English. I take it you're not from around here either."

"No, we came here very much the same way you did."

"So, you were also caught up in a freakish lightning storm," Cobb said.

"A freakish lighting storm. Yes, I guess you could call it that. Although, calling it a time storm might be more accurate," Lionheart responded.

"How did you do that? I mean, kill all of those creatures so quickly? What kind of guns are those?" Cobb asked.

"They are lightning guns and are very effective against what the locals call Tiesposka," Lionheart said.

77. HAVING FRIED THE SWORM of deadly creatures, Captain Lionheart introduced himself to Captain Cobb as he helped him up.

"Tiesposka, that's what the man we saved called them," Hadley said.

"Yes, the literal Russian translation is Death Cat. From what I have discovered, I have the impression they are the result of a breeding experiment to produce a new form of weapon by the local authority," Lionheart said.

Petrov stepped up to the prisoner and spoke to him in Russian. After a short conversation, Petrov turned around. "His name is Leonid Averin. He says he is a veterinarian from Moscow who helped with the cross breading experiments here. He said after he first declined an offer to come here, his sister was abducted, and he was told she would be safe as long as he cooperated. She was killed two days ago when they were both caught trying to escape."

"What was his plan?" Lionheart asked.

After speaking to Averin again Petrov responded, "He says there is an airfield to the north where the airship Alexi from Moscow brings in supplies periodically. His plan was for them to stowaway on the ship to reach Moscow, but he says Moscow isn't safe. So, from there they were planning to make their way to St Petersburg, then on to Sweden," Petrov responded.

"Captain, judging by your fire power, you seem advanced to us. We have a very serious problem. My first officer has been stung by one of those creatures. We came out here hoping to take a dead specimen back to our doctor to see if he can work out an antidote. She won't last much longer. Can you help us?" Cobb asked.

"We can certainly try. Take us back to your ship," Lionheart said. As both groups started to walk back, Lionheart continued. "My crew and I are in the same position you are in Captain. Our ship is stranded here just as yours is. We approached you because I think we might be able to help each other get out of here," Lionheart said.

At that moment, Averin stumbled forward and collapsed unconscious.

"He must be totally exhausted after his ordeal," Cobb said, as he motioned for two of his men to pick him up and carry him along.

78. THE RUSSIAN AIRSHIP ALEXI, Averin spoke of, was the only contact (other than the train shipments of mineral ore) the Siberian Kings had with the outside world.

"Where did you come from?" Cobb asked, as he continued his conversation with Lionheart.

"Actually, we came from Arizona. But the question for both of us, and anyone else who may have encountered that storm up there, is not so much where, but when. We are from what on your calendar would be late 19th century. Your maiden voyage is history to us. That's how we knew about you and your ship," Lionheart said.

"Well, if I had not witnessed the power of your lightning guns, I would have had a hard time believing you. If our voyage is history to you, can you explain the airship that killed nearly a third of my crew?" Cobb asked.

"That part of your voyage was never officially documented. But there were vague accounts from surviving crew members that suggested the Minerva made a brief visit to the mid-18th century. We were able to, at least in part, determine what happened on your voyage. Before the last storm brought you here, the Minerva appeared in the skies above a great battle that was waged in the eastern Mediterranean. So far, it was the greatest battle in recorded history. The casualties from it numbered in the millions. The ship that attacked you was a German air wolf." Lionheart said.

Later, when both parties reached the Minerva, it was late in the afternoon and a thick ground fog had set in. Lionheart could see the Minerva had suffered serious damage. From the look of it, he thought Cobb was overly optimistic about flying it again. Had it not been for recorded history and Hermes children's book, Lionheart would have thought the Minerva was finished.

"If you can save Raleigh, I'll do anything I can to help you," Cobb said, as they climbed aboard.

For a brief second, Lionheart's face had light up with recognition. He quickly tried to hide his response. Lionheart heard the name of Raleigh before.

"We have an extensive medical facility on my ship, and they will do everything they can," Lionheart said. They met with Doctor Pike and saw Raleigh. She was almost dead. "I'll arrange to have her taken back to our ship. We also have the resource to restore your ship and resupply your hydrogen," Lionheart said, as he motioned for two of his people to come over. They gently moved Raleigh on to a stretcher. Lionheart reassured Cobb they would do everything they could for Raleigh. When Pike saw Averin, he knelt down to examine him. "This man is badly hurt. I'm afraid he won't last long," Pike said, as he got to his feet.

"Captain, can we also take him with us?" Petrov asked. Lionheart agreed. In spite of Pike's objections, Cobb assured him both of them would be in safe hands. As Cobb watched Lionheart's man carry Raleigh and Averin away into the fog on a stretcher, the strangest feeling came over him. It was as though he would never see Raleigh again. Having made the deal with Captain Lionheart to have the hydrogen restored, Cobb countermanded the order to dismantle nonessential parts of the ship.

It wasn't long until Raleigh and Averin were aboard the Onyx Tower, in the medical bay. Lionheart ordered Averin to be placed in isolation to prevent him from seeing any part of the ship. When Connors learned Lionheart brought another Russian and Minerva's first officer on board, she became curious as to why. She felt it would have been better treating them off-sight. Thornton was also curious. Lionheart came in to see how her condition was. He saw both Connors and Thornton when he arrived in med bay.

"Captain, I'm curious why you had the sting victim brought on board. You know from what we have determined so far, the sting of the Tiesposka is always fatal. There is little I can do for her except to make her comfortable, just as the Minerva's doctor was doing." Connors said.

Lionheart motioned for both of them to step into Connors' private office. He closed the door after they entered. "I can't explain this to either of you, but just before we departed from Earth, I received special instruction from one of my associate's, Mr. Terra. When his secret cargo of re-generation pods was being loaded on to the ship, he told me the time would come when we would encounter a woman called Raleigh. He told me she would be critically ill and that I was to use one of the pods to re-generate her. Terra said it was absolutely essential that I do this," Lionheart paused for a moment.

"Connors, I want you to prepare the re-generation chamber. We must have Raleigh back aboard the Minerva in 24 hours. Let me know when you have everything ready. I'll be in my quarters," Lionheart said, as he left. Somewhat stunned by Lionheart's orders, Connors and Thornton briefly stood motionless looking at each other.

"Well, let's get to it," Thornton said, as they left the cabin.

Alone in his quarters, Lionheart looked out at the fish swimming in the dark waters outside his window. Of all the places he intended to visit, he never imagined his ship would wind up being partly submerged in a cold lake somewhere in Western Siberia. The water outside was just above freezing. Terra's unusual request regarding Diana Raleigh prompted a search into history that led him back to the Minerva's maiden voyage. Having studied Minerva's history in detail, at least as much as he could, he wondered if he would be able to fulfill the portion that involved him and his ship, as told of in Hermes' book. There was a knock at the door. "Enter," Lionheart said, as his thoughts were interrupted. It was Thornton.

"Captain, we told Ms. West about Raleigh, and she came across something in the ship's library that I think should be brought to you attention. While reviewing Raleigh's history, Ms. West discovered something that strongly supports the possibility Raleigh went through the re-generation process," Thornton said.

"Go on," Lionheart said, as he turned and gave his full attention.

"According to history, the Minerva departed on its maiden voyage in May 1555. Approximately six weeks later, Cobb, Raleigh, and what remained of the crew were rescued off the coast of Honduras. Six years later, in July 1561 both of Raleigh's parents were murdered by pirates while sailing off the Somali coast. After the incident, Raleigh sought and got vengeance on everyone involved with the murders. This pursuit also led to and included some people in very high places around the world, who were using the pirates as a front to carry out their dirty work. It was later recorded that she caught up to the last of her adversaries in 1586, 25 years after this started," Thornton said.

"Go on," Lionheart said, after Thornton paused.

"It was later reported, the decedents of some of the people she tracked down came to America looking to avenge the deaths of their family members. They were not successful. The last of them were reported killed in 1598. Our records in the ship's library say Diana Raleigh was born in October 1528. Now bear in mind, at this time, 1598, Raleigh's age would have been 70, 43 years after our encounter with Minerva. What caught my attention was in 1626, 71 years after our encounter, a legend known as 'Diana, Lady of the Forest', began in Southern Louisiana. According to history, it all started when the town of Houma was raided by a gang of outlaws who killed several townspeople and took hostages in the attack. They fled into a remote area deep in the bayou. Later, the hostages came out unharmed, with a story that a lady of the forest killed off their captors, a lady they called Diana. Since then, other stories have circulated about some angelic entity deep in the forest that has saved people lives and protected others from harm," Thornton paused again.

"Terra told me, after a person goes through re-generation, they are no longer completely human, but rather a hybrid of plant and animal. Their new body is said to be much stronger and have greater endurance then the original, and it begins to age at a much slower rate. So much so, that the subject may need to move around to conceal their true age. However, Terra also told me he believes, without going through another re-generation, in time (approximately every 50 years) the subject's plant side will start to become more dominant, even to the point where it will seek to merge with all surrounding plant life. He said it was only a theory of his. However, if Terra is correct that would mean Raleigh would start changing in 1605, 50 years after re-generating. She must have gone into hiding in the Louisiana bayou when she realized what was happening to her." Lionheart explained.

"If this Lady of the forest is indeed our Diana Raleigh, there must be some truth to Terra's theory. It also means that right now, at this moment of time we are in, 1627, there is another Raleigh living on the far side of the world," Thornton said, just as there was a knock at the door.

"Enter," Lionheart said.

"Everything is ready Captain," Connors quietly said, as she entered.

"Very well, start the procedure as soon as possible. Also, make sure the skeleton from her original body is removed before she wakes up. We will explain to her the procedure has increased her strength and living capacity, but I think the less she knows about the true nature of it, the better. Send for me after she is dressed," Lionheart said.

"Yes Captain," Connors said as she left the cabin.

The dimly lit, oblong re-generation chamber had a low ceiling. There was a central raised platform that ran almost the entire length of the chamber. Its only entrance was a door at one end. There was a small window on the opposite wall. Wearing gloves and protective clothing, Connors and her assistant, Dr. Dorian entered the chamber and made their way up opposite sides of the platform, carrying a metal cylinder between them. A look of caution came over their faces as they gently sat the container down and opened it. Small puffs of cold gas escaped from the contents inside. Inside was what looked like a large, thick, bare animal skin rolled up. After carefully pulling it out of its container, Connors and Dorian rolled it out flat across the platform.

"So, this is what immortality looks like," Dorian said.

"I know, this is the first time I have actually seen one of these," Connors responded.

It was actually a specially treated skin section that came from the giant Lunar mushrooms. The mushrooms were known to have mysterious re-generation properties. Before Lionheart departed from Earth, one of his associates, Dr. Terra, gave him 60 re-generation pads to take on this voyage, thinking they would help ensure the chances of his survival no matter what they encountered.

Connors and Dorian left the chamber, taking the empty case with them. Moments later, they returned with two other medical crewmen carrying Raleigh. With great care, they place her down directly on the pad. Based on her experience with other crew members that had been stung, Connors could see that Raleigh would have lasted only another hour or so before dying. Before starting the procedure, Connors withheld Raleigh's pain medicine. Raleigh's face was beginning to contort with pain as she was starting to wake up. After a moment she became relaxed again as her body came under the influence of the rolled out pad beneath her. She fell back into a deep sleep. Connors and Dorian lifted the sheet that covered Raleigh. Everyone left the chamber and the door closed behind them, sealing the chamber up tight. A moment later came the sound of air rushing around as the air pressure dropped slightly to remove any contaminates in the chamber. Now it was just Raleigh, alone on the pad. Now the process would begin.

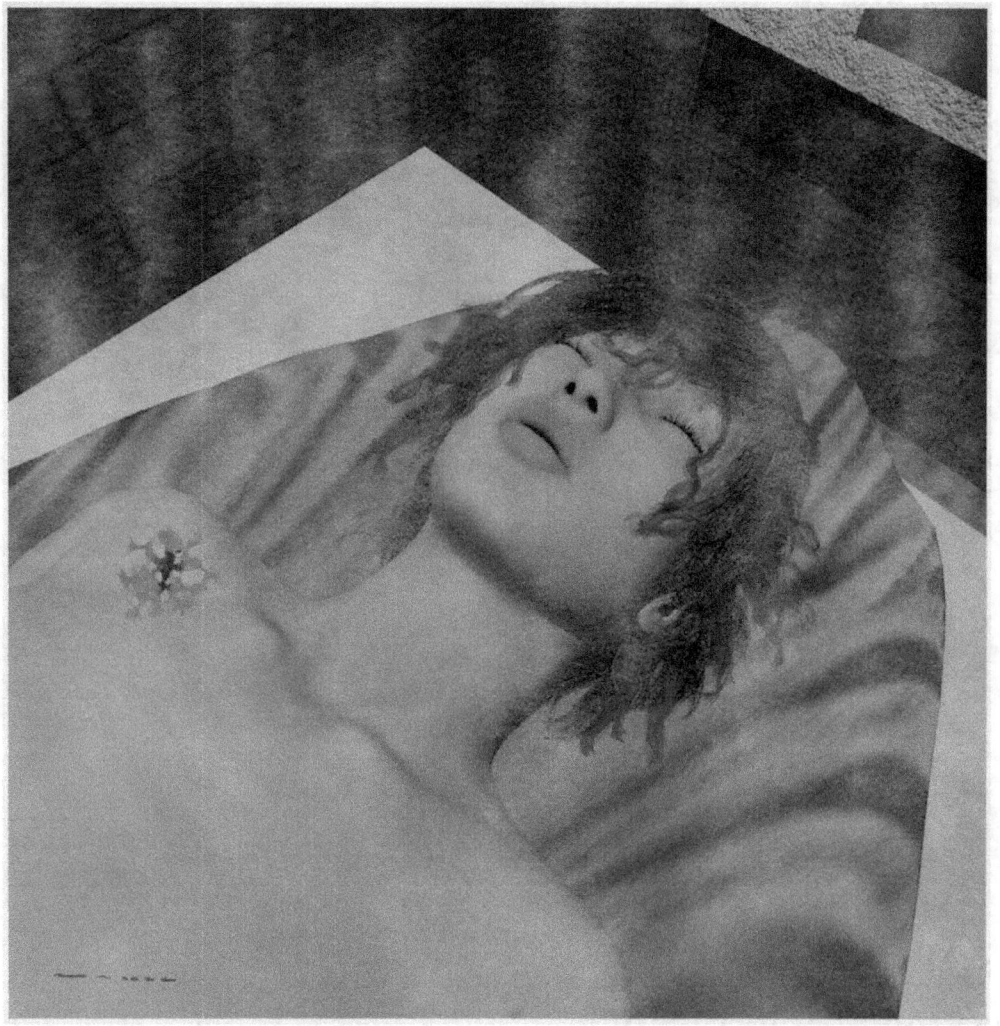

79. ONCE PLACED ON THE PAD, to undergo the re-generation process, Diana Raleigh no longer felt the horrible pain in her right shoulder where she had been stung. The vapers coming off the lunar mushroom pad quickly lulled her into a deep sleep.

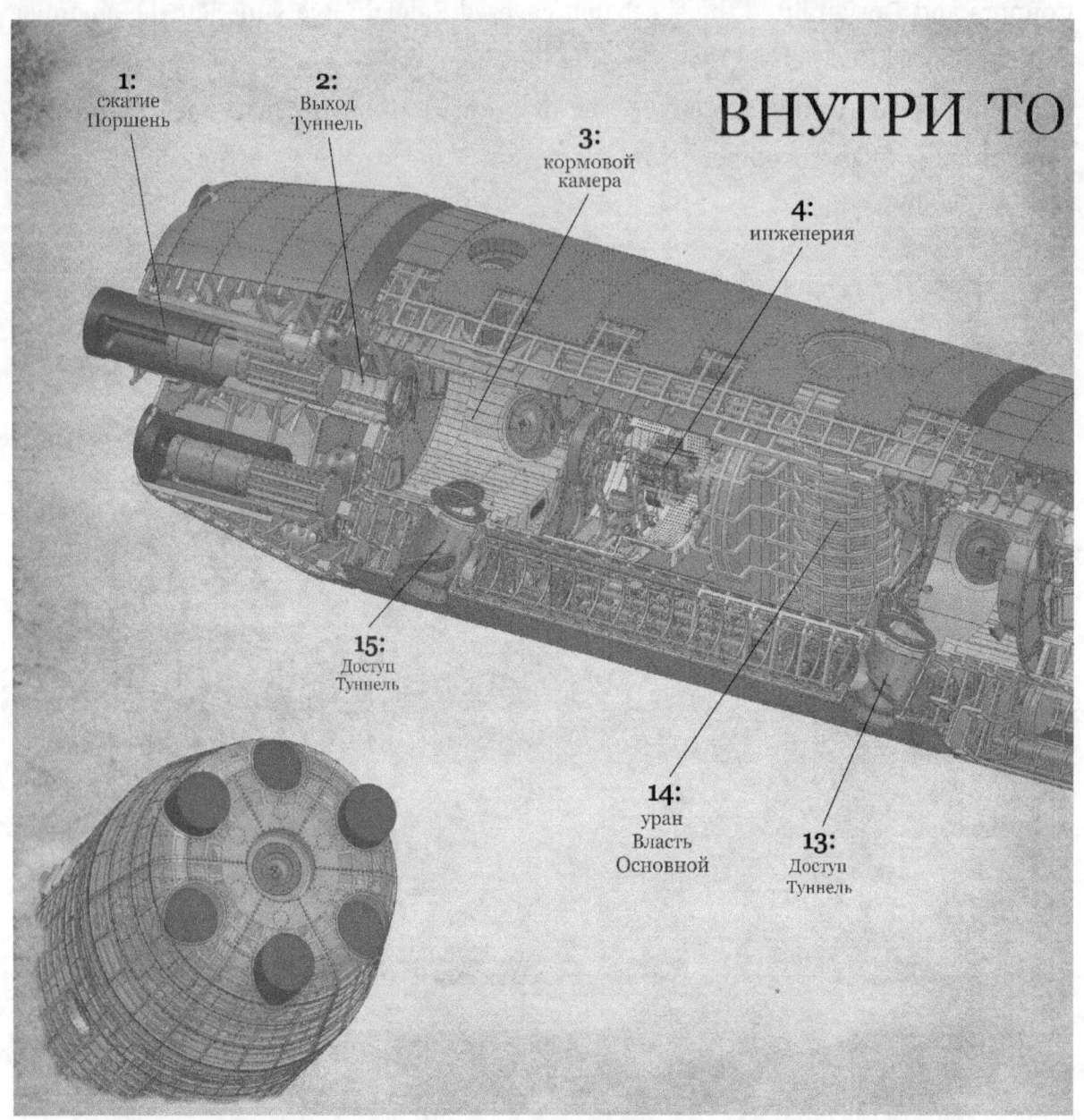

1:
сжатие
Поршень

2:
Выход
Туннель

3:
кормовой
камера

4:
инженерия

ВНУТРИ ТО

15:
Доступ
Туннель

14:
уран
Власть
Основной

13:
Доступ
Туннель

80. INSIDE THE IRON MOLE: **1.** compression piston, **2.** exit tunnel, **3.** Aft Chamber, **4.** Engineering, **5.** Helm, **6.** Caterpillar Drive, **7.** Cone Control, **8.** Cutting Cone C, **9.** Cutting Cone B, **10.** Diamond Tip, **11.** Access Tunnel, **12.** Navigation, **13.** Access Tunnel, **14.** Uranium Power Core, **15.** Access Tunnel. [Ivanov Scroll 1 of 23]

ЖЕЛЕЗО КРОТ

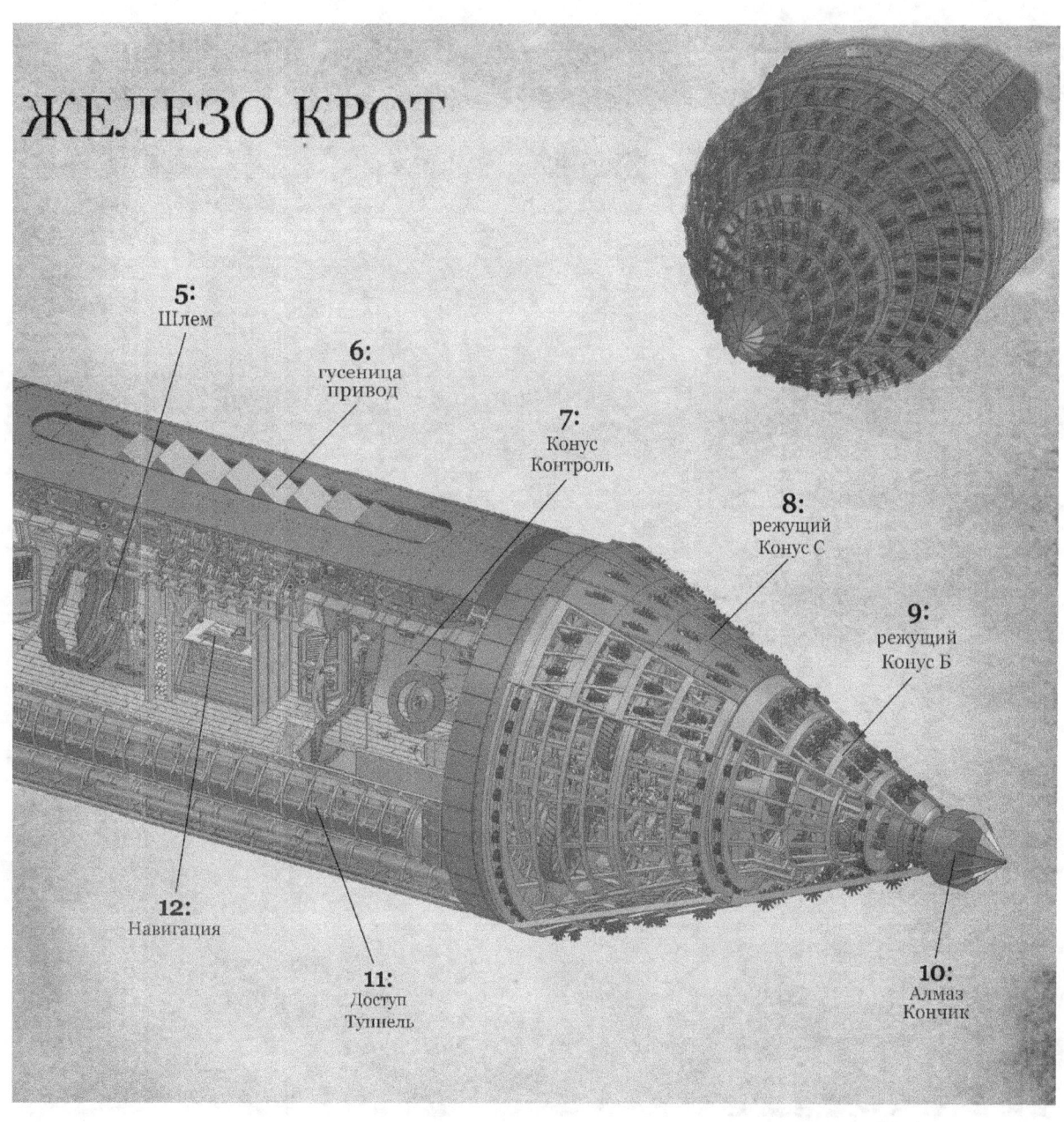

5:
Шлем

6:
гусеница
привод

7:
Конус
Контроль

8:
режущий
Конус С

9:
режущий
Конус Б

12:
Навигация

11:
Доступ
Туннель

10:
Алмаз
Кончик

167

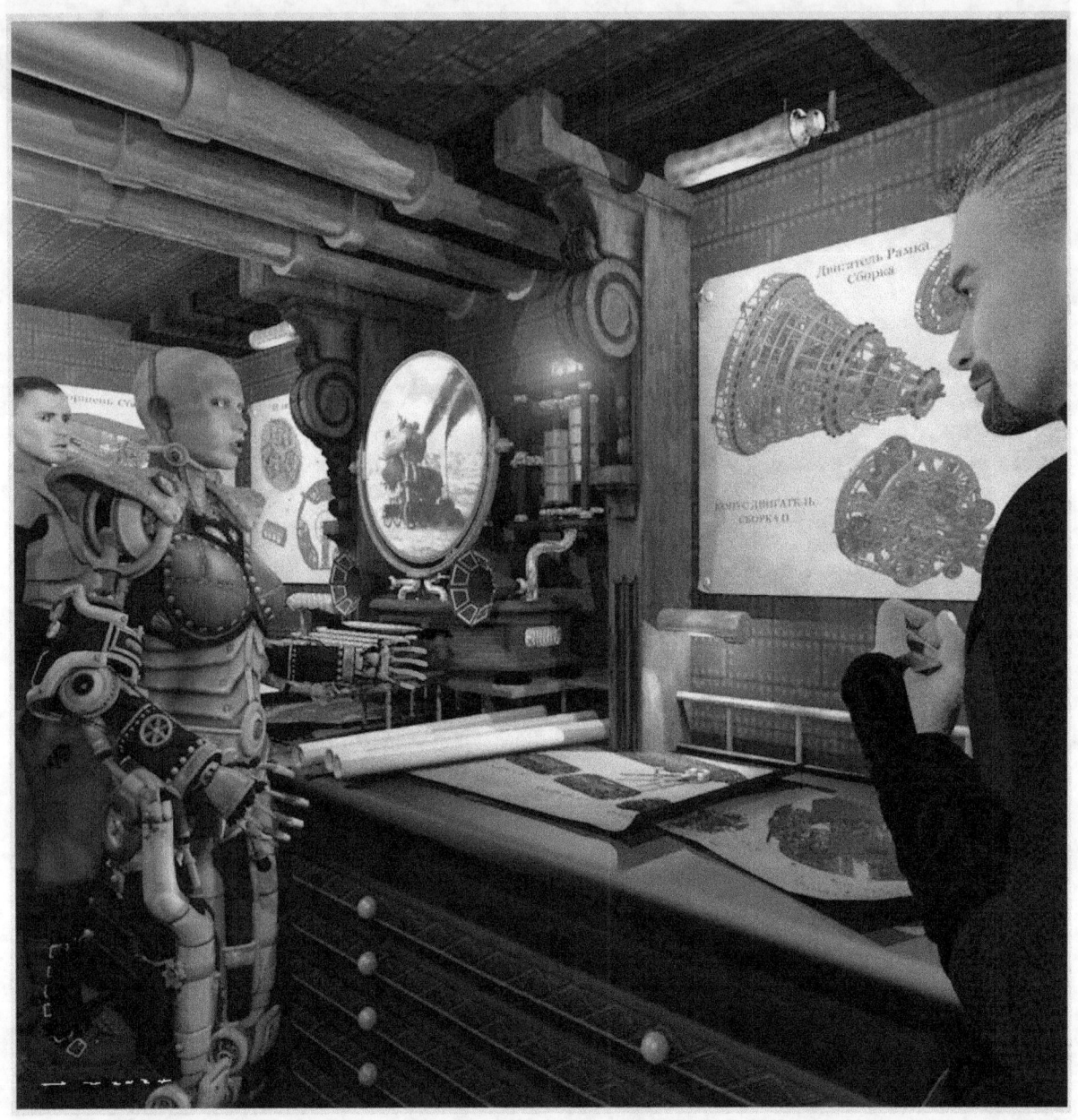

81. WEST, PETROV AND THORNTON examined the Ivanov's material in the Onyx Tower's library. The assorted material contained maps, photographs, and scrolls. They were interested in any information on the iron mole's power source.

МОДУЛЬ 3

Власть Основной и инженерия

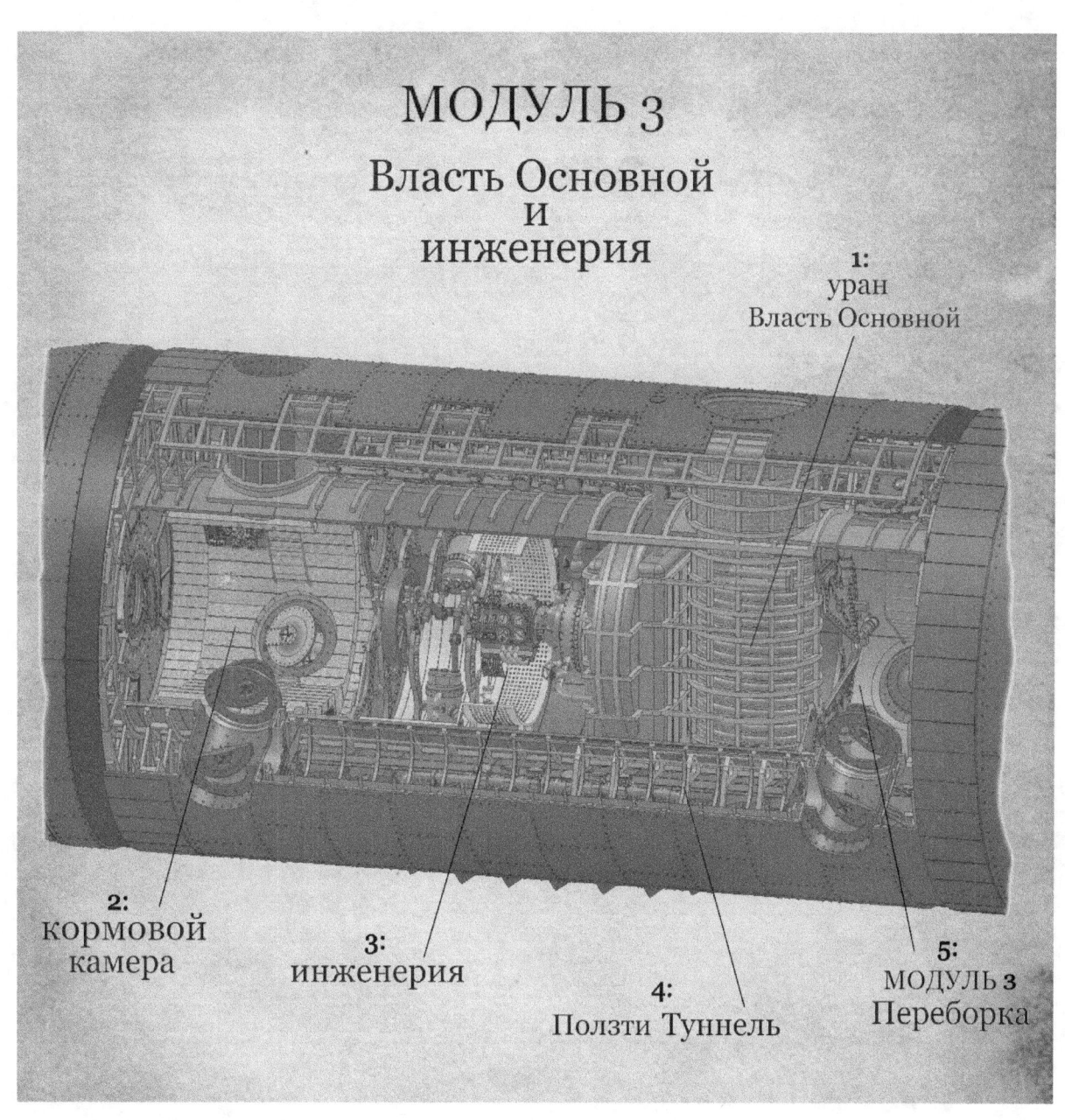

1:
уран
Власть Основной

2:
кормовой
камера

3:
инженерия

4:
Ползти Туннель

5:
МОДУЛЬ 3
Переборка

82. MODULE 3 POWER CORE AND ENGINEERING: 1. Uranium Power Core, **2.** Aft Chamber, **3.** Engineering, **4.** Crawl Tunnel, **5.** Module 3 Bulkhead. [Ivanov Scroll 17 of 23]

Власть Основной

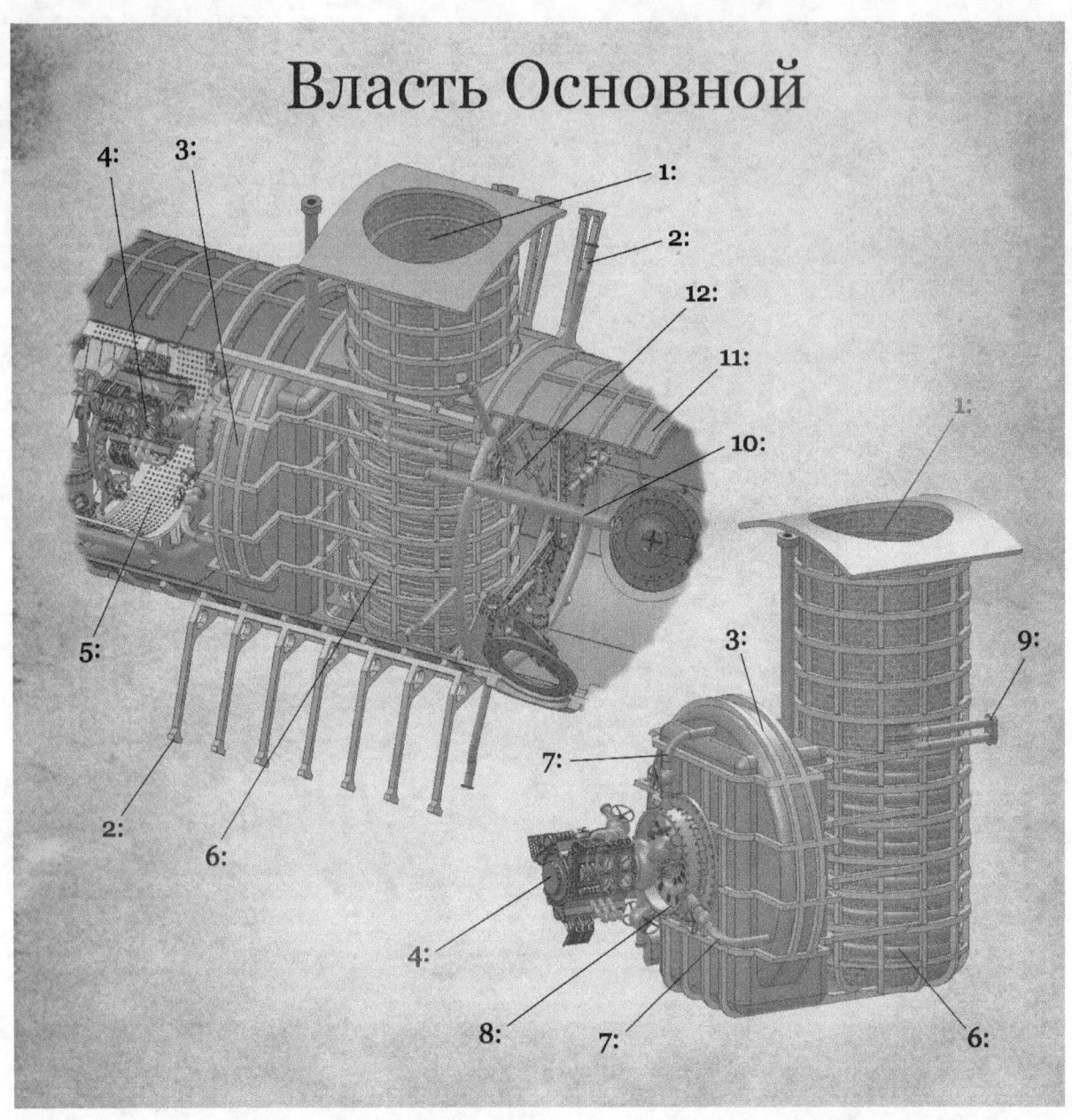

83. **POWER CORE:** **1.** Power Core Chamber **2.** Support Brace **3.** Generator Turbine **4.** Core Power Control **5.** Engineering Control Floor **6.** Core Steam Coils **7.** Turbine Steam Line **8.** Generator **9.** Core Steam Exit **10.** Core Exit Steam Line **11.** Inner Hull **12.** Power Core Bulkhead. [Ivanov Scroll 18 of 23]

Thornton, West and Petrov met with Lionheart in the wardroom. The luminary table projected an image of the tower in the lake and the surrounding area. As they stood around the table, Petrov started to explain the plan to re-start the Onyx Tower's power core.

"Captain, after speaking further with Ivanov about the details of the subterranean steamships, more specifically their power source, Thornton, West and I have worked out a possible plan of how we might be able to tap into it," Petrov started.

Not saying anything, Lionheart motioned to him to continue.

"When Ivanov escaped from the land steamer, the scrolls he was carrying contained a wealth of information. They contained maps and detailed drawings of their subterranean steam ships. He was also carrying several photographs. I believe he wanted to show proof of what was going on out here," Petrov said.

"Sir, according to Ivanov, the subterranean steamships have a cylindrical chamber in which molten ore is poured into. The ore chamber is much like a crucible except it can be completely sealed and has water coils wrapped around it to power steam pistons throughout the ship," Thornton said.

Still, even a large crucible with molten ore would cool too quickly to drive one of these iron moles for very long. At best, the ships power would last only long enough for the ship to bury itself. Please go on," Lionheart said.

"That would be true except Ivanov said, before the molten ore is poured into the chamber it is mixed with something Master Krnobov invented. It is known only as Medusa oil. They call it that because anyone who has looked directly at its blue light died hours later," Petrov said.

"Medusa oil, it sounds more like a mixture of active uranium. My God, those idiots are mixing active uranium with molten ore! That would explain the appalling death rate and the uranium rays we detected earlier!" Lionheart said.

"Captain, we think we can use this to our advantage. Petrov has figured out a way to rig one of the E-M-2 portable generators with a heat conducting rod that, when is inserted into the iron mole's core, could produce enough power to help initiate the startup power needed for the tower," Thornton said.

"You have worked this out Petrov?" Lionheart asked.

"Yes Captain, in fact my people are modifying one of the generators as we speak," Petrov said.

84. JUST PRIOR TO THE IRON MOLE'S DEPARTURE, an ore mixed with active uranium is poured into its crucible chamber. By the time this photograph was shown to Lionheart all five men shown had passed away from uranium exposure.

"So, how exactly do you plan to get one of our generators off the ship when it's submerged and over one these iron moles?" Lionheart asked.

"Well Sir, that's where the Minerva comes in," Thornton said, as he paused for a moment, leaning on over luminary table. "As you can see, this is a detailed close image of our current position."

"You mean here in the middle of a lake," Lionheart said.

"Yes- Now right down here is the Minerva. Captain Cobb tells me with our help, his ship will be ready to fly in 24 hours. Since our arrival, our meteorologist, Barnes, has tracked the local weather patterns in the area. According to Barnes, in the upper fog layer, there has been a slight wind current in a north easterly direction. Now when the Minerva lifts off from its position down here," Thornton said, as he pointed to a 3D image projected on the table, the wind current should carry the ship over the lake. As it does so, it will pass almost directly over the Onyx Tower and then it will continue on over an area where the iron moles have been sighted," Thornton said, as he pointed to the other figures on the table.

"So, when the Minerva passes over the Tower, it will grapple the modified generator with a tow line and carry it over the iron mole area?" Lionheart asked.

"Precisely! A long power cable will be attached to the generator," Thornton said.

"It all sounds good except for one thing. How do you know if there will be any iron moles present when the Minerva passes over that area?" Lionheart asked.

"Ivanov told us one of the iron moles is scheduled to surface in the area approximately located here 24 hours from now," Petrov said, pointing at a projection of an iron mole on the table.

"How would he know that?" Lionheart asked.

"The digging schedules for the moles are planned in advance. Ivanov says he helped plan the schedule," Petrov said.

"It's going to be cutting it awfully close. We have to get Raleigh back to their ship just before then. Getting into the iron moles core, did Ivanov give you any details on exactly what is required to do it?" Lionheart asked.

"Yes, he did Sir. Ivanov's description was very thorough. Once the mole has surfaced, we know exactly what to do."

85. **THE PLAN** as shown on the Onyx Tower's luminary table in the wardroom. **Lower Left:** The Minerva lifts of from its position. **Center:** The Minerva retrieves a generator as it flies over the Onyx Tower. **Upper Right:** The Minerva lowers the generator over and into an iron mole that has just surfaced.

"What about the land steamer that dropped it off? Shortly after the iron mole surfaces, it is sure to come back, "Lionheart asked.

"Yes sir, about that, we were thinking about creating a weather diversion," Thornton said.

"Are you talking about using the Blue Stone?"

"Yes, Based on what Ivanov told us, we think the land steamer will come from this direction to retrieve the iron mole." Thornton said pointing down at the map. "The plan is to have Elston and Moss here on the ridge with the Blue Stone."

Lionheart said nothing as he leaned back and took a deep breath. "You know- I've never been completely comfortable having that thing on board. That was part of Dana's little bag of tricks she insisted I take with me on this journey. She told me it was retrieved from some distant world she once visited through one of her portals. We intended to use it only to create precipitation in the event we landed on a desert planet and needed water. I still don't know if using it to create a storm as a diversion is a good option," Lionheart said.

"It was not our first choice, but it was the only one we could think of that would not draw too much attention to ourselves," Thornton said.

"We will have to use it as far away from the site of the iron mole as possible. A nearby storm could threaten the Minerva. I agree with using it. There is one other thing that bothers me. What about this airship, the Alexi? If it is flying nearby, it could report what is happening to their forces out here," Lionheart said.

"I can't be sure but both Ivanov and Averin said it was mostly used for flying between here and Moscow only. There is no guarantee it won't be in the area," Thornton said.

"Well, we will just have to risk it. We really have little choice. It is this or nothing. Good work you two," Lionheart said.

As the hours passed, the air pressure in Raleigh's chamber slowly returned to normal. It was almost a day later. The re-generation process was nearly complete. Raleigh had been kept under constant observation. Connors and Dorian quietly entered and removed the skeleton left over from Raleigh's original body. Two hours later Raleigh began to awaken.

86. **WHEN DIANA RALEIGH'S RE-GENERATION WAS OVER:** Dr. Conners managed to remove her original skeleton before she woke up. Raleigh's wound was completely healed. She later noticed her body was free of all the little scars from previous injury's in past years.

As Raleigh sat up, she was somewhat startled to find herself in a small stone chamber completely undressed. She looked down at the place where she had been stung. There was no trace of any wound. As she took a deep breath, she felt strong and alive with a newfound energy. As she continued to look down at herself, she noticed all the little scars she had collected over the years were gone.

The chamber door opened. Connors entered, carrying Raleigh's clothes.

"Who are you and what is this place?" Raleigh asked.

"I'm Doctor Connors and you were near death when they brought you here. This is a medical chamber where we were able to treat your condition. Here are your clothes. You can come out after you've dressed. The Captain wants to meet you," Connors said.

Later, Raleigh met with Connors and Lionheart. Without revealing too much about themselves, they explained their situation and the alliance they made with Captain Cobb. Lionheart and Connors were careful not to reveal any details about the regeneration procedure, but Raleigh was told the procedure that saved her life also made her physically superior, and she was now aging at a much slower rate. In the years ahead she would have to take steps to conceal her true age.

Hadley was the first to spot Lionheart and Raleigh as they came out of the fog. Cobb was greatly relieved. When he saw that Raleigh had been completely cured, he considered himself in Lionheart's debt. During the time Raleigh had been away, with the help of some of Lionheart crew, the Minerva was almost fully repaired and ready to fly. In place of the gas filled rooster that had been torn off, a gas bag fabricated by Lionheart's crew had been attached in its place.

For Cobb, the hardest part was waiting for the time when Lionheart would call upon him to use the Minerva to retrieve something. He didn't have to wait long. When Raleigh was brought back, Lionheart said it would be less than a day until Minerva was needed. Cobb was given the general details of Lionheart's plan. For Cobb, the plan was simple, all he had to do was lift off to a low altitude no higher than 500 feet [152.4 meters], fly his ship over the lake passing directly over Lionheart's ship and drop a cable where a small piece of cargo would be attached, carry it over to an area on the far side of the lake, lower and release it under Lionheart's direction, and that was all. Just before he departed, Lionheart said he would return in less than 24 hours.

While the Minerva was being refurbished, Lionheart left some crewmen behind armed with lightning guns to protect Cobb and his crew in the event of another attack from the Tiesposka. They did attack several times. During one attack they flew around Raleigh but showed on interest in her. No one knew why. Cobb and Hadley believed it was because she had already been stung and had some sort of immunity. When Connors got news of it, she knew it was because the Tiesposka creatures sensed Raleigh was a plant. They have no interest in plants. When Raleigh was alone, Hermes approached her. At first, he said nothing as he looked her up and down. "My God, you look, and sound just like her. I'm glad to meet you. In the years to come you will become a part of everything around you," Hermes said. He nodded slightly and left. Not knowing how to respond, Raleigh just nodded back.

The Face of Evil

It was quiet in the Onyx Tower's medical bay after Lionheart was away returning Raleigh to the Minerva. Ivanov got up off his bed and began to slowly make his way around the area. Nurse Conley and Ratchet saw him and offered to help, but he only smiled and waved that he was ok. They thought it was good for him to get out of bed and could see that he was walking very carefully. They went back about their business as Ivanov continued to shuffle along slowly.

Ivanov heard another Russian had been brought on board. As he looked around, he made his way over to the individual intensive rooms. The door to each one was closed but he could see in through the small window of each door as he passed. Ivanov stopped at the one Averin was in. Ivanov could see that Averin was asleep. Ivanov slowly opened the door, stepped inside, and stood at the foot of Averin's bed. Averin started to slowly wake up. He didn't recognize the silhouette of the person standing at first, then his face had a look of horror when he realized who it was. Averin started gasping for air as he started to have a heart attack. Ivanov just stood there with a slight grin on his face. With one last gasp Averin whispered "Krnobov!" just before he died.

Responding to the alarm, Conley and Ratchet ran as quickly as they could to Averin's room. When they got there Conley tried to revive him as Ratchet called for Docter Conners. They were unable to save Averin. When it was over Conley recalled they had not seen Ivanov since they first saw him earlier. She started to wonder if he was ok. She was relieved when she looked in on him only to find him sleeping.

87. LESS THAN A DAY AFTER RALEIGH'S RETURN, Lionheart appeared, just as he said he would. Thornton, Ross, and Quinn were with him. After they boarded the Minerva, Captain Cobb gave the order to lift off. Cobb was relieved. He didn't want to stay in Russia any longer then he had too.

Cobb gave the order for everyone to be as quiet as possible. Even though a heavy fog covered most of the landscape, he didn't want to alert the Russians to his presence. A light breeze was blowing to the east. As they drifted along, the low misty fog continued to cover much of the ground below. As Lionheart stood out on the helm deck, his attention was focused on a small handheld device that he quietly spoke into. He couldn't be sure, but he thought he could hear the faint sound of a distant engine coming from the horizon. After a moment or two, he dismissed it as his imagination.

"We are on the correct heading. The breeze should carry us directly over the lake and the... "Thornton paused as he corrected himself "...our ship."

"Very good Thornton," Lionheart said.

They were moving at a very low altitude of only 300 feet or so. As they floated along, it was quiet. After a while, they would hear the sound of water lapping against the lake shore from below. A short time later, they could see the upper spike of the Onyx Tower sticking up above the fog layer.

"We're getting closer," Thornton said.

"Is that the top of your ship?" Cobb asked.

"Yes, please drop the grappling cable now," Lionheart said.

A cable was lowered from Minerva. Cobb and Raleigh became very curious about what Lionheart's ship was like. They had the impression they were flying over a tall building rather than a ship. Something under the fog layer below grabbed onto the cable and began to pull it tight. The Minerva stopped drifting. Down below, Petrov secured the modified generator to the cable. A power cable was also secured to the generator that would unroll as the generator was pulled away.

"Captain, Petrov has secured the package and released the cable. We can continue on," Thornton said.

The Minerva dropped slightly as the cable was hoisted up away from Lionheart's ship. Once again, the Minerva began to drift along in the breeze. As soon as it was clear from Lionheart's ship, some ballast was dropped to compensate for the added weight of the generator they were carrying.

88. **UNDER THE GUIDANCE OF LIONHEART,** the Minerva came upon the Onyx Tower through the heavy morning fog.

As Petrov watched the generator disappear into the fog above, he hoped they would be successful. The Onyx Tower was almost completely out of power. They had less than an hour left. Portable lanterns had already been distributed throughout the ship. When he returned to engineering, Ms. West was there.

"Mr. Petrov, if I may, I would like to remain and monitor the startup procedure," Ms. West said.

"Of course," Petrov said.

"Captain, we are right on course," Thornton said, looking at his compass.

After a short time, they could hear the sound of water lapping against the shore as the Minerva started to pass over land again.

"If Ivanov's information is accurate, the area where the iron mole will surface isn't much further," Thornton said.

As they headed away from the lake shore, it became quiet again.

"Captain, it's time for Elston and Moss to start the diversion," Thornton said, looking at his watch.

"God help us," Lionheart said, quietly, as he nodded.

Clouds of black smoke from the land steamer revealed it's presence long before it entered the narrow gorge to reach the iron mole's retrieval area. The steamer's helmsman gave little attention to the rocks and boulders that were easily crushed under the wheels of the grand juggernaut. No one noticed the small remote controlled vehicle nestled among the boulders ahead. The vehicle was small, about the size of a child's wagon.

Watching closely from a side ridge, Elston and Ross stayed low to avoid being seen.

"It's time. Let's go." Elston said as they both backed away for the safety of the amphibian behind them. Once inside they signaled the small remote vehicle to open. Ross hoped the conducting rods positioned near the amphibian would keep the lightning strikes to a minimum. The top of the remote vehicle opened revealing a blue luminous sphere that pulsed with sparks of energy. Almost at once a light breeze began circling around the gorge. The breeze became wind as it grew stronger.

No one on the steamer noticed the light from the pulsing blue sphere. Their gaze was on the swirling dark clouds above that seemly appeared out of nowhere. A sudden bolt of lightning struck the steamer's pilot house, then another and another. Large splinters of wood and metal were blown off with each strike. Any crew that were outside quickly tried to get to safety inside the steamer. The captain ordered the steamer to a full stop until the sudden storm subsided. The pilot house became engulfed in fire as the lightning strikes continued. The heavy rain all around did little to tame the fire. The captain gave the order to abandon ship as the fire began to spread below the pilot house.

Lightning struck the amphibian as well. Elston and Ross could see that the land steamer had stopped and was now on fire. They were both taken back by the power of the blue stone. They also knew Lionheart would be disappointed. Their orders were to stall the land steamer, not destroy it.

"Well, that could have gone better. Signal Thornton that the land steamer has stopped. Will give a full report later," Elston said.

"Captain, Ross has signaled the land steamer has stopped. Our little diversion is working," Thornton said.

"Good. We are almost over the iron moles exit point," Lionheart said.

"Do you plan to capture this ship?" Cobb asked.

"No, we just want to borrow some heat from its engine," Lionheart responded.

Cobb and Raleigh just looked at each other.

"Captain, I have concerns about the storm off in the distance. It might be best if we secure the ship," Raleigh suggested.

"Yes, but not just yet," Cobb responded.

"Well, at the very least, we should weigh anchor. At this rate, the Minerva will drift past the intended site," Raleigh said.

89. **THE POWER RELEASED FROM THE BLUE STONE** proved to be far more devastating than anyone realized. It's brief exposure released a miniature thunderstorm that was so intense the land steamer caught fire and it's captain ordered abandoned ship. When Dana first presented the stone to Lionheart, she told him the stone was actually a powerful semi-solid containment field that held a tiny piece of a neutron star. After his experience, crewman Elston felt it would have been fitting to have its little vehicle built to resemble the Ark of the Covenant.

185

"You're right. Reduce altitude by 100 feet, when we are about to be over the area Captain Lionheart wanted. Have the aft harpooner fire a grappling line," Cobb ordered.

"Captain, I'm getting a signal from Larson directly ahead. He reports the ground is starting to quake where the iron mole is about to surface. His team is in position and ready to act as soon as it does. We are almost upon them," Thornton said.

"Now! "Cobb said to Raleigh. A ground grappling hook fired from the aft. Larson and his team below heard the harpoon cannon fire. The Minerva was almost directly overhead.

"Good, it would seem the information from Ivanov was accurate," Lionheart said, as he leaned over the railing and looked over at the thick fog below.

Down at the site, Larson and his men were not exactly sure where to stand. The subterranean steamship was about to surface, but no one knew exactly where. At that moment a low, muffled engine noise could be heard. All of them could feel the vibration increasing under their feet. Everyone backed away as the ship began digging itself out. The iron mole's large drill point was the first to break thru, followed by the ship's counter-rotating cone rings. The rotating rings cut through solid rock with minimal effort. It made Larson think of a large whale plunging out of the water, and like the whale, a good portion of the iron mole was above the ground when it fell back down onto it. The weight of the initial impact caused a shock wave in the ground that almost knocked Larson and him men over. Not far from the iron mole was a steep cliff of large boulders. For a moment, Larson was afraid the shock would start an avalanche. As the iron mole came to rest on the surface, they could hear the engines shutting down as the massive cloud of dust began to settle. The rock-cutting rings began to slow and eventually stop. Larson and his men quickly ran to the hatches. Not wasting a second, they opened them, tossed in small canisters of leaking gas, and closed them tight again.

90. **AS THE IRON MOLE SURFACED,** Larson and his men were waiting.

Everyone wore suits for protection against the uranium rays from the iron moles core.

"That will keep the crew asleep for a short while," Larson said, as he stepped away.

There was a problem. The iron mole's core hatch was on the underside of the ship. It would have to be rolled over before Petrov's generator could be inserted. The news was quickly relayed to the Minerva.

"Captain Lionheart, if I may suggest, the nearby storm has caused the breeze to pick up. It may be possible to roll the iron mole by attaching cables from our ship and deploying its sails. As you can see, the breeze that brought us here has increased to a light wind. It may be enough," Raleigh suggested.

"It sounds like a good plan. Let's give it a try," Lionheart said.

Several cables were secured to the iron mole and the grappling anchor was released. The wind was getting stronger, but it wasn't enough. The iron mole only rocked back and forth a little. After that, Larson had a cable attached to each of the amphibian vehicles, and the combined effort only caused the iron mole to roll slightly. For a moment the effort seemed futile.

Everyone was so preoccupied with the situation that almost no one noticed a swarm of Tiesposka was about to close in on their position. At first there was a yell from Minerva's crow's-nest. Then the swarm was upon them. Larson had a small group, led by crewman Mullin, armed with lightning guns in the event of an attack. At first the swarm attacked Larson's group. Looking down, everyone on the Minerva could see the lightning below, lighting up the fog as they fired into the creatures. Moments later, the remaining creatures departed and flew up to the Minerva. Lionheart only had two men armed with lightning guns, but it was enough to kill the remaining swarm. As before, they had no interest in Raleigh. During the attack, one of the large boulders tumbled down and struck the iron mole, causing it to roll over a little.

After the smoke cleared from the battle, Mullin suggested an avalanche of the large boulders from the slope nearby might be enough to roll the ship over. Larson was reluctant at first, but agreed, as it was their only option. The gunmen were careful to position themselves to run fast once the avalanche started. Only seconds after lighting their guns up, they all ran as hard as they could to dodge the incoming boulders. Even though he was clear from the ship, a huge boulder was following Mullin. Seeing he couldn't outrun it, he turned and fired. The seconds seemed like minutes as the boulder was almost upon him. Seeing what was happening, his men close by concentrated their guns on the boulder and fired. Just as Mullin was about to be crushed, the bolder exploded into a cloud of smaller rocks that rained down on him. His men ran over as the dust and smoke cleared. They pulled him up out of the rubble. He was shaken up but ok. Looking back at the iron mole, Mullin smiled as he could see that it had rolled over and its core hatch was now on top.

"Captain. Signal from Larson, the iron mole is upright. We can start the operation," Thornton said.

"Thanks Thornton. The fog is clearing below. I think I can see it from here," Lionheart said, leaning over the rail.

Larson and two of his men wasted no time in getting on top of the iron mole. The generator was lowered from the Minerva until its pointed spike was just above its intended target. Using grappling hooks, Larson and his men maneuvered it directly over the core. Larson signaled Minerva to release the generator. As it fell, its lower spike penetrated all the way through the core cover. The protective cap at the top of the spike blocked any harmful uranium rays. After a moment, the generator came to life. Seeing that it was secure, Larson and his men slowly backed away.

Standing in the power control center of the Onyx Tower, Petrov could see the ship was receiving power. The batteries to the startup system were beginning to recharge.

"Captain, message from the Tower. Petrov says the system is charging Sir. Uranium levels are minimal. The generator shield is working," Thornton said.

"What now Captain?" Cobb asked.

"Now we use a small flame to start a fire. You can release the grappling anchor. After we are out of the immediate area my men and I will depart," Lionheart said.

A short time and distance later Lionheart and his men entered Minerva's elevator.

"It's been a pleasure working with you Captain. Again, I can't thank you enough for Raleigh," Cobb said as he shook Lionheart's hand.

91. LIONHEART'S GENORATER POWERED UP after being inserted into the iron mole's core. Even though Larson and his men were wearing protective suits, they stepped back slightly after they finished to avoid any possible exposure to the core's deadly uranium rays.

"The pleasure was mine Captain. It isn't often one gets the opportunity to meet a historic legend," Lionheart responded, shaking Cobb's hand.

"I wonder what will happen to us next," Raleigh said.

"Well, according to history, you made it back," Thornton said.

After Lionheart and his men were on the ground, they waved and watched as Minerva's elevator cage was pulled up and its grappling anchor released. A moment later, water ballast was dropped from above. Lionheart and his men dodged the water, as they watched the Minerva ascending. Within moments it was up and moving toward the southern horizon. Minerva rose higher in the sky. Soon it was moving west across an open valley of clouds. Cobb looked out at the sun and took a deep breath. He was relieved to be on his way again, but wondered where their next destination would be. After all they had been through, he wanted to return to Texas.

"We are going to see Lionheart one more time," Hermes said. At first his presence at the helm startled everyone. He was so quiet when he approached no one noticed him.

On the ground below, Lionheart and his men watched as the Minerva sailed out of view.

"That has to be the first time I witnessed a ship sailing straight into the history books. I wonder what our history will be," Thornton said.

"Well, there's only one way to find out. Let's get back," Lionheart said. A short time later, they joined Larson's party. Uranium levels were still at acceptable levels, but just to be safe, Lionheart, Thornton and the others split up and quickly boarded the amphibians.

"Open a channel to the Tower," Lionheart commanded.

"A channel is open to Petrov now Sir. We have maintained constant contact since the operation started," Ross said.

"Mr. Petrov, how far along are we?" Lionheart asked.

"95 percent. We are almost there Captain. I take it all went well with Minerva?" Petrov asked.

"Yes, the Minerva is headed back to its own century. We will head back to the tower as soon as we are through here."

"Ok Captain, just a few minutes more and will be at 100 percent."

"Very good Petrov," Lionheart said.

At the Onyx Tower everyone was so preoccupied with the ship recharging that no one noticed another airship had appeared on the horizon and was closing on their position.

Ms. West suddenly raised her head and looked away from the console she was sitting at. It was as though there was someone in the room speaking to her. "Mr. Petrov, there is what appears to be an airship of unknown origin approaching from the northeast," she said.

At first, Petrov was surprised, then he remembered Ms. West was directly tied into the ship and wondered if the airship was the Alexi that Averin spoke of earlier.

"Mr. Petrov, sensors have picked up what looks like an airship closing in on our position," Helmsmen Quinn reported over the com.

"Is it the Minerva?" Petrov asked.

"Negative Sir, this one is much larger. It is now at five miles and closing. At its current rate, it will be over the Tower in approximately three and a half minutes. The ship appears to be Russian. Sir, I think they have been alerted to our presence."

"Petrov, what is going on?" Lionheart asked.

"Captain, we are at 97 percent and there is another airship closing in on our position. I think it's the Alexi," Petrov said.

"Mr. Petrov, We have a visual on the ship. Its markings are defiantly Russian Sir. Doors on the under hull are opening up. Sir, I think they mean to bomb us!" Quinn said.

"Captain, we think the Alexi airship intends to bomb us!" Petrov said.

"Well at least the tower is built to withstand a direct hit from a uranium bomb," Thornton said.

"It's not the Tower that concerns me. It's the possibility that a bomb blast could sever the cable connection before the ship is fully recharged. Without power there is nothing we can do to stop it," Lionheart said.

Minutes later, the Tower was being bombed. In spite of all the violent explosions that hit the upper dome, they only rocked the Tower slightly, and had little effect. No one inside could even hear the bomb blasts. The power cable survived the first pass. When the smoke cleared there was no sign of any damage. The airship turned to make another pass. Once again there were many violent explosions around the upper dome. This time the cable connection was blown apart and the cable itself was shorting to the Tower's hull. Lionheart and the others could hear the sounds of the distant bombardment.

During the bombing no one noticed Ivanov left his bed and was no longer in Med bay.

"Petrov, what is happening to my ship?" Lionheart asked.

"Captain, you need to cut the generators power! The severed power cable is shorting to the tower's hull!" Petrov said.

"Larson, kill the generator!" Lionheart commanded.

"Captain, something is wrong. The generator is overheating! It is starting to melt!" Larson said.

"If it melts it could rupture the shield under it and expose the iron moles core!" Thornton said.

"Get the dark powder," Lionheart said.

"Captain, are you sure? If you use it, some of the iron mole's crew could be killed." Larson said.

"If they have an exposed core, they will all perish," Lionheart said.

"Mr. Larson, the generator has melted into the shield sir! It only a matter of time before the shield fails!" Mullin said.

"We don't have any choice. Use the dark powder now Larson," Lionheart said.

"Sir, uranium levels are rising! The shield is starting to fail!" Mullin said interrupting.

92. DESPITE THE VIOLENT EXPLOSIONS that hit the upper dome of Onyx Tower, they only rocked the Tower slightly, and had little effect.

"Aye sir!" Larson said, as he held up an unusual gun with a long glass barrel.

Larson warned everyone to get further away from the iron mole's core. He estimated that he was approximately fifty yards from it. Before leaving the Tower, Ms. West had adjusted the gun to fire a level of the sub-atomic black power to offset the energy of the iron mole's uranium core. Larson took aim at the iron mole's core and yelled out "Powder in the hole!" as he pulled the trigger. No wasting a second, he turned and ran as fast as he could in the opposite direction.

The newly formed invisible sub-atomic particles they called "black power" penetrated the iron mole at the speed of light. They were attracted to the energy of its uranium core. Once at the core, the particles stopped, and their influence began to slowly expand outward in a sphere from the core's center absorbing energy as it went. The sphere of black powder's influence became visible as it expanded out beyond the iron mole's exterior. When Larson and his crewman saw it, they were even more fearful because direct contact with it would be immediately fatal. It would literately suck the life out of them. The sphere grew just large enough to engulf the iron mole's core. Then it faded and was gone. Ms. West had calculated the right amount of power to offset the core's volume. When it was over the deadly uranium ore had been reduced to harmless graphite powder. Unfortunately, inside the iron mole, an engineer who was near the core and inside the area of the dark powder's influence was killed when his life energy was also neutralized.

"Captain, the core and powder have neutralized each other," Larson said.

"Ok, good work Larson. Mr. Petrov, report. What is the status there?"

"Captain, the ship is undamaged, however when the charging cable was severed, we were at 98 percent of the minimum charge needed to initiate startup," Petrov said.

"Mr. Petrov, cut all power to the rest of the ship then initiate start up, What we have will have to do. This is the only chance will have to get out of here," Lionheart said.

"Yes, but Captain, if this fails... "

"We have to go with what we have Petrov, Lionheart out," Lionheart stopped and took a deep breath. "Mr. Larson, open all of the iron mole's hatches. The outside air should revive the crew. Signal Elston and Ross to close the Blue Stone and return to the Tower. There is nothing more we can do here. Let's get back to the ship."

93. LARSON AND HIS CREWMAN RAN FOR THEIR LIVES as the black powder's sphere of influence became visible. Fortunately, it stopped and faded away when the iron mole's core was neutralized. Unfortunately, it killed the iron mole's engineer inside who close to the core at the time.

When Elston and Ross closed the Blue Stone, the storm began to dissipate quickly. The land steamer had burned almost to the ground by this time. The surviving crew had long since abandoned ship running off back in the opposite direction. Elston and Ross wasted no time leaving the area.

With the weather clearing, the Russian airship Alexi continued to search the area. They had reports of another airship.

"Well, it's this or nothing. Cut all power to the ship except for engineering. We'll try to initiate startup," Petrov said.

Ms. West sat at her console with the usual expressionless face.

"Aye sir, I hope this works. Chamber is at vacuum. Initiating magnetic pulse field. Field strength is at 20 percent and rising. 30 percent, 40... ", crewman Jacobs said as power levels rose to increase the pulse field. When 98 percent was reached, Petrov turned on the plasma injectors. The fusion ring was somewhat unstable at first. It was simply bleeding off to much energy to sustain itself. For a brief moment, it looked like it was going to stabilize, then it started to break up.

"We can't maintain it sir! We simply don't have enough power!" Jacobs said.

"Aye, that's what I was afraid of. Well, we might as well shut down. At least we have enough auxiliary power to run the ship for a few more days." Petrov said.

Before Jacobs could kill the power, the plasma ring suddenly stabilized.

"Sir, the plasma ring, it's coming back up! It's coming back up to full power!" Jacobs said, as he nervously pulled his hand away from the kill button and closed its cover very carefully.

In a small access way behind the energy chamber, Ivanov stood alone in the shadows. The small metallic disk he placed on the outside chamber wall completely disappeared when the power came up full.

"During the procedure, Ms. West monitored something unusual. With a direct feed of ship's information into her mind, she could literally see the plasma energy ring and the magnetic fields around it. At the exact moment the ring increased power and became stable, she saw an unknown conduit of energy being injected into the ring. Its source wasn't from any of the chambers six injectors, but rather a blank area on the wall.

"Captain, it worked Sir. The reactor is running at nominal power. The ship will be fully charged in a few minutes," Petrov said.

"Nice work Petrov. We are almost back," Lionheart said.

Unknown to anyone, Ms. West got up and made her way to the access way on the far side of the reactor. She stood alone in the shadows exactly where Ivanov had been only moments earlier. There was no sign of anything unusual. She closely looked at the exact spot on the reactor wall where the unknown stream of energy came into the chamber. She reached out to touch the area very slowly. Just as she did there was a static discharge. She registered 157 volts. She touched the wall again. This time there was nothing. Ms. West logged the observation of the unknown energy source in her mind, thinking it was possible she might later acquire further information to explain the event.

All the away teams arrived back at the Tower. Lionheart was eager to get underway as soon as Petrov confirmed that it was safe to do so. He knew the Russians would come to investigate the portion of the Tower that was above water. After Engineering, Lionheart made his way to the bridge where Thornton was waiting. Lionheart felt a sense of accomplishment. He suddenly realized how uneasy he had been for knowing that he and his crew would have an historic encounter, and if it would unfold just as the one, he read about.

"Captain, full power has been restored to the ship. We can leave at any time Sir," Thornton said.

"Very good. Blow the ballast tanks and initiate internal drive engine," Lionheart commanded. Thornton repeated the order into the com.

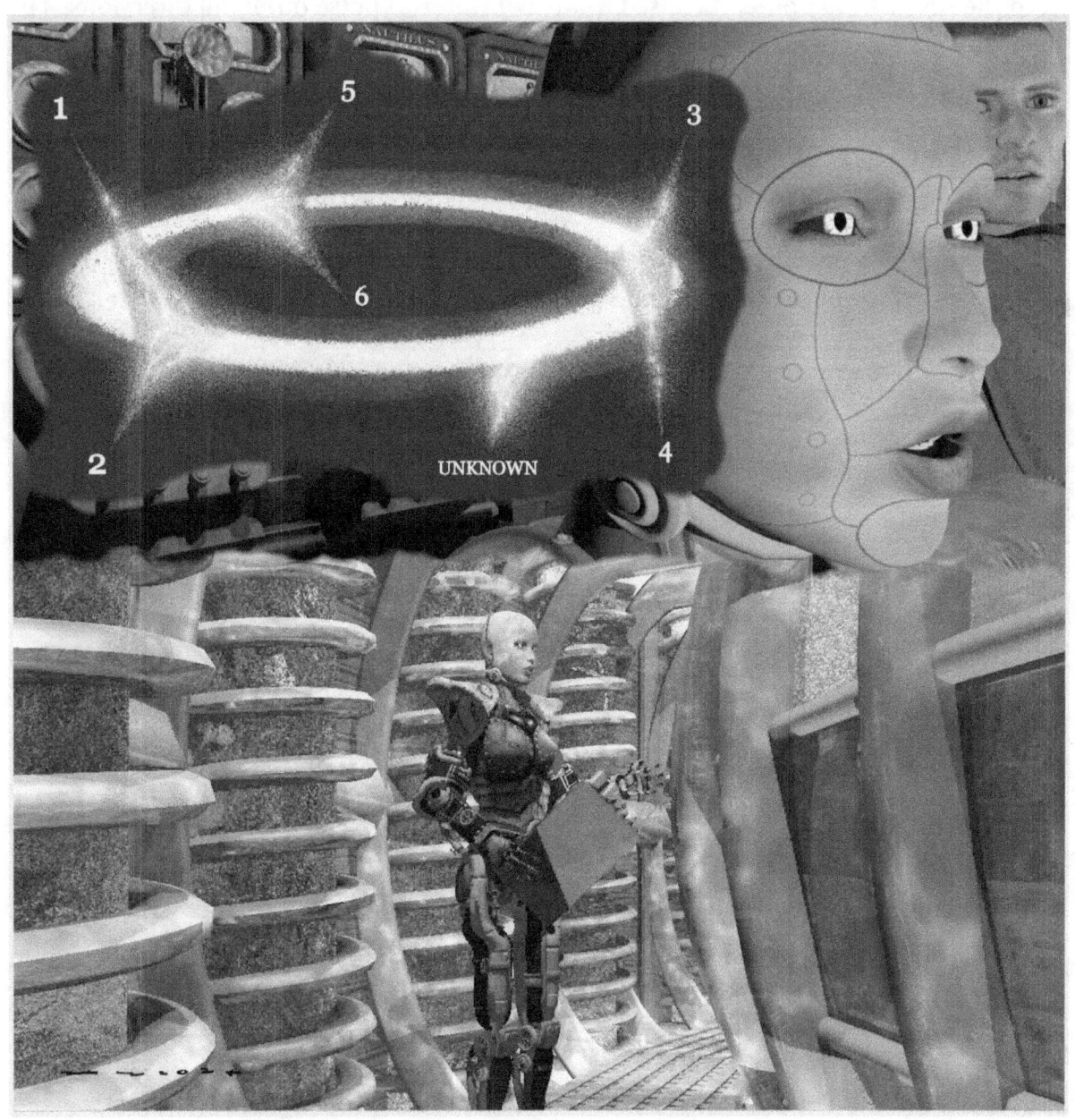

94. THE PLASMA ENERGY RING was visible in the mind of Ms. West. West could also see energy being injected from an unknown source. Moments later in the tower's power room, West stood at the exact spot where the unknown source of energy had been injected into the plasma chamber and was unable to find anything.

Up on the lake's surface a moment later, came the sound of a deep pulse emanating from the tower's top dome. It caused a wave of water to pulse out in all directions. The energy pulse was so strong it caused a faint vibration on Minerva's deck that made the crew nervous even though they were several miles away. A second pulse came soon after, followed by another, then another until they came a regular intervals, faster and faster. After a moment, they began to fade and soon could no longer be heard. Elsewhere on the lake, just over a mile away, a lone fisherman was overjoyed from having fish jump out of the water into his boat when the sounds from below started.

"Internal drive engine online, Captain," Thornton said.

"Mr. Thornton." Lionheart paused for a moment. "Raise the Tower. Take us up," he commanded.

"Aye Captain. Mr. Quinn, bring the Dana engine to 1.05 gravity," Thornton commanded.

"1.05 gravity, Aye Sir," Quinn repeated.

The lone fisherman on the lake was Alexander Tvardovsky, a renowned artist under the employ of Count Vladislav. With a boat filled with fish, he was still filled with joy. He only fished as a hobby and considered a catch of six fish to be a good day. Now, with a boat filled with them, he started throwing some of them back. As he rowed back to the lake shore, the occasional deep pulse of sound coming from the water continued to make him nervous. The morning fog had reduced visibility to a hundred feet. Another sound started. It was the sound of distant waterfalls. It was faint at first, then it steadily grew louder and louder until it was almost deafening. Tvardovsky became frightened. He thought the dam had burst. Looking toward the direction of the sound, Alexander could see a domed, spiked tower rising out of the fog. He stood up to get a better look. Soon other, smaller towers near its base began to appear. He was so overtaken by the sight; he didn't notice the wave coming toward him. When it hit, he was knocked out of the boat. Before he could climb back in, a second wave hit. Floating in the water, he could see a grand Tower with waterfalls cascading off as it rose up into the sky.

95. THE LONE FISHERMAN, Alexander Tvardovsky, was overwhelmed by the sight of the tower as it rose up out of the lake. He paid little attention to the wave that knocked him out of his boat.

96. **ALTHOUGH SOMEWHAT HORRIFIED** by what had just happened, Tvardovsky was influenced by what he had witnessed. So much so, he briefly departed from making his beautiful jewel studded eggs and created a golden jewel studded Tower. Centuries later, that tower became the prize in a bet between two powerful brothers to see who would be the first to reach the Moon.

Higher and higher the Tower rose until it disappeared into the fog layer. Alexander didn't realize his mouth had been wide open. He was starting to gag on water he was swallowing. He swam his way back to his boat, climbed in and started bailing water. After the Tower was gone, the lake once again became quiet and serene.

As Lionheart and the others looked out from the bridge, the morning sunlight felt good. It donned on Lionheart that the crew had been under cloudy, gloomy conditions the whole time they were there.

"Captain, the airship that bombed us earlier is closing in on the Minerva," Ms. West said.

"Mr. Quinn, stop our accent, hold altitude, and get us within lightning range of that ship!" Lionheart commanded.

"Aye Sir!" Quinn responded.

"I was hoping to get out of here with the least amount of disturbance. I can't allow the Minerva to be attacked," Lionheart said quietly.

On the Minerva, Raleigh was the first to see the Russian airship closing on their position.

"Captain, another ship is closing fast from astern!" Raleigh said.

"Dammit! Not again! The last time this happened we lost a third of the crew!" Cobb said as he looked astern.

Several gunmen tock up position on the bow of the Russian airship and began firing on the Minerva. Cobb ordered everyone to take cover. After being struck by a bullet in the right shoulder, Hadley stumbled back and fell over the railing. As he did so, he held on to the rope he was winding. The spool of rope began to rapidly unwind as he fell. Raleigh ran over and grabbed the rope with her bare hands. She was quickly pulled to the rail. The rope was still running through her hands as she wedged herself against the rail. The rope slowed and eventually stopped as she tightened her grip. She kept her concentration on Hadley as she single handedly pulled him up and back on board. As she did so, two crewmen were shot and wounded as they tried to get to her.

Eventually she got Hadley to safety then pulled the other two crewmen to safety while still under fire.

As the Russian airship was just about to come along side to fire their cannons, there suddenly came a deafening clap of thunder and lightning, striking it from the far side. In an instant, its rudder was completely blown off. Within seconds, the Alexi was hit with more lightning strikes, blowing its hull into small pieces that fell to the earth. With the hull blown away, its severed balloons floated upward. Cobb, Raleigh, and the rest of Minerva's crew stood motionless as they watched the cloud of debris fall into the fog layer below. Seconds later, they could feel a faint vibration in the deck. Cobb feared that the Minerva was about to be hit by lightning.

"Lionheart!" Hermes said as he pointed at some dark clouds on the starboard side of the ship. The vibration on the deck began to increase. A spike came up out of the clouds. It was soon followed by a large dome. It turned out to be the top of a tower. Then other spikes attached to smaller domes appeared around the tower's base. The smaller domes and towers were part of a grand structure. Overwhelmed by the sight before them, Minerva's crew stood there with their mouths open.

"My God, it's a floating Castle!" Cobb said with his mouth still hanging open.

"*It is Lionheart. The Children of the Tower returned to their kingdom in the clouds,*" Hermes whispered to himself quietly.

The floating tower stopped for a moment. Then it rose up into the sky and was gone. The sight of it was burned into everyone's memory. It took several minutes for the crew to realize they still had a ship to fly. After attending to the wounded, Raleigh returned to her cabin. Through all the excitement, she didn't think to look at her hands. After grabbing a rope with a 180 pound, falling man at the other end, stopping the fall, then pulling a man back in, her hands should have been bleeding badly at the very least. Yet, during the event, she experienced no pain. As she looked down at them, there was no sign of any wounds or skin irritation. She did, however, have the sensation of two irritable splinters in her side. She wondered if they came from the wooden railing. As she looked down, she noticed two small holes in her vest. She unbuttoned it and opened her shirt. She was surprised to find the back end of two bullets sticking out of her side. As she pulled them out, she felt the relief one would get from having a splinter removed. "What did they do to me?" she quietly said to herself, as she dropped them on the desk in front of her.

It was now early evening. Not being able to sleep, Raleigh returned to the helm. The moon was coming up.

97. WHAT DID THEY DO TO ME? That's what Raleigh asked herself when she pulled two bullets out her side like they were nothing more than splinters.

98. **AFTER STOPPING THE ATTACK,** the Onyx Tower ascended into space.

Back in Space

"Captain, the Moon is coming up," Thornton said as the tower entered outer space.

"Helmsmen, lay in a course for the edge of the solar system. Let's try this again. Once there, we'll ride the space wave to Proxima Centauri b," Lionheart commanded.

"Aye sir. Course laid in," Quinn responded.

As Lionheart looked back, and the Earth and Moon getting smaller and smaller, Thornton came up alongside saying "Captain, you know we are now leaving the Earth in 1627, 253 years before we did the first time," Thornton said.

"I know. Ms. West insisted that we do not attempt to follow the Minerva in an effort to get back to our own time. Somehow, I have a suspicion she has some insight into our future," Lionheart said.

"Did you ask her why?"

"I did, and all she said was that I would understand in due time, whatever that means. Either way, I trust her completely. I know we are not in our own time, but I suppose it really doesn't matter, not really. In the scheme of the cosmos, 253 years has almost no meaning. If we are successful in establishing settlements, they will be further along when the rest of the Earth catches up to us. It's time to head for the stars," Lionheart said.

"I suppose, just as long as we don't have to return to the Earth for any reason to get help," Thornton said.

"Well Petrov, we found out the Russian legend of the Siberian Kings is true. We only saw a part of it. I'm having West and the ship's cartographer, McRandel document everything we came across," Lionheart said.

"Aye Captain, what we saw was more than I care to see. I wonder if there is anyone who will really know the full story behind Count Vladislav's empire," Petrov said.

Later, Lionheart was alone in his cabin looking out at the now distant Earth and Moon. "It's good to be back in space again." He wondered why Ms. West was insistent that he make no attempt to follow the Minerva into another "Time Storm" (as he now referred to it) in an effort to return to the approximate time they were taken from.

The first stop would be the Totem Valley on Proxima b. Now Lionheart was going to see it again, two and one-half centuries before he saw it the first time. As he thought further, he wondered what Ms. West had fabricated down in the ship's factory. When questioned, he got the same response that he would understand in due time.

99. AS THE ONYX TOWER WAS LEAVING THE EARTH, Lionheart realized the sight of his ship leaving would be recorded in a book.

It was now early evening. The Minerva was cruising along in a peaceful breeze. Standing on Minerva's deck, Hermes stood motionless, still thinking of the great floating Tower. The peace of Minerva's surroundings was short lived. The wind was picking up. The clouds all around were getting dark. Hermes looked at the dark horizon ahead.

"Well Hermes, do you have any predictions?" Cobb asked jokingly.

"There is a dragon coming, a very powerful dragon, but fear not. The dragon was a man once, a descendent of Lionheart's crew," he said quietly. As always, he turned and left for his cabin.

Cobb was sorry he asked. The wind continued to pick up. Cobb could see another storm was coming.

"Oh no, not again," Cobb said quietly to himself, as the storm approached. Yet he and the rest of the crew knew they would have to go through it at least one more time in order to get back to 1550. As Cobb and Raleigh looked back, they could see that a distant time storm was forming not far behind the ship. With a tunnel like formation made of blue glowing lightning clouds, its features were now unmistakable. They knew sooner or later they would have to pass through another time storm.

"Captain, the time storm appears to be following us. It seems to be closing in unusually fast," Raleigh said.

"We can't outrun it. Well, we knew we would come across one eventually. Everyone, brace for another storm!" Cobb yelled.

Before anyone could react, the time storm was once again upon them. The intense winds rocked the ship violently. The glowing blue tunnel clouds appeared. Cobb hoped the new repairs would be enough for the ship to survive the storm. At one point, the deck listed over, and Hermes slid from a cabin doorway and bounced hard against the railing. Reacting with almost lightning speed, Raleigh grabbed him and pulled him back to his cabin.

"The last storm tock us into the future. This one is taking us into the past, but we will only be here for a short time. The one controlling the storms doesn't want us here." Hermes said as Raleigh returned to the bridge.

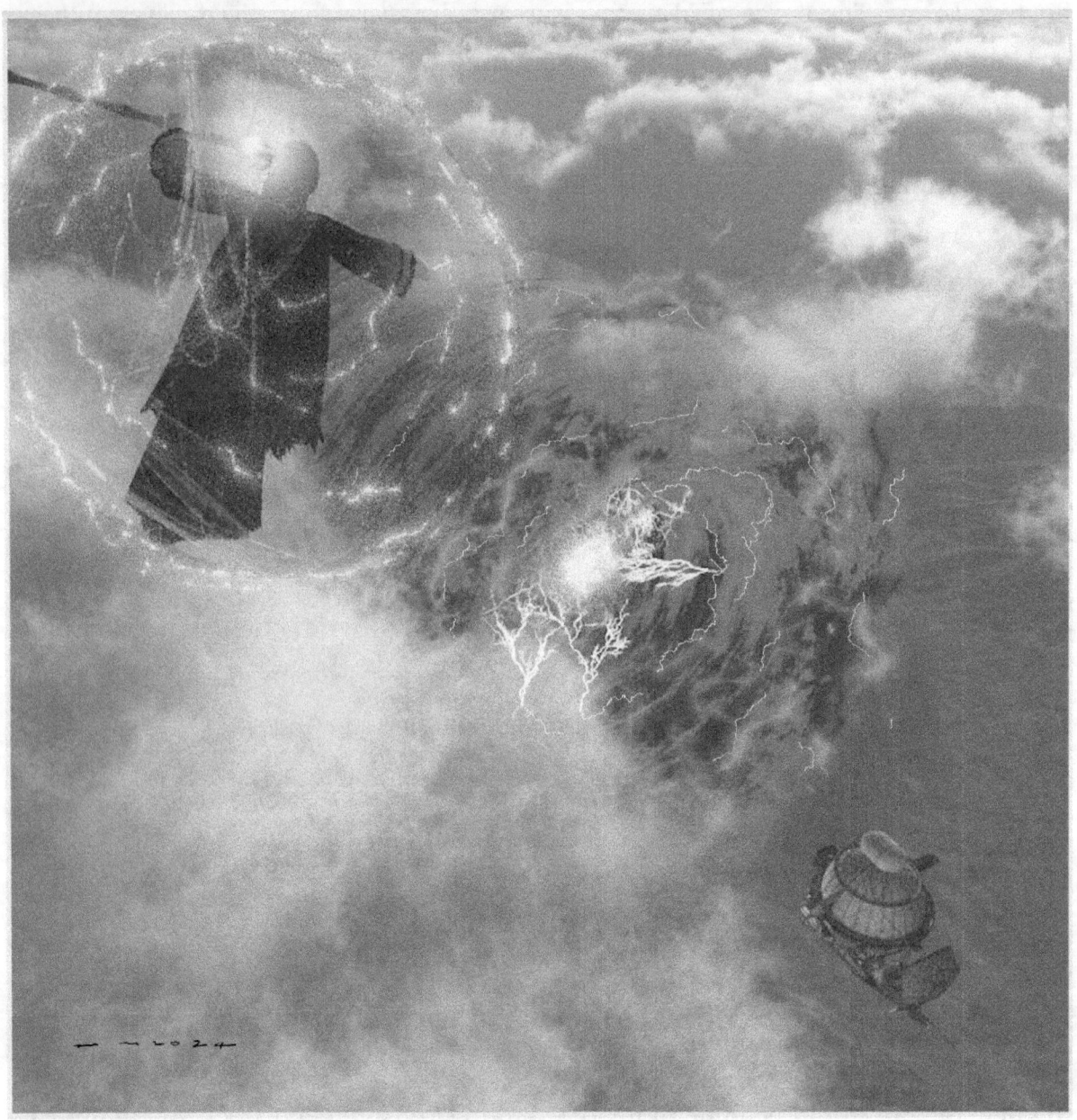

100. **HERMES LATER REVEALED THE TIME STORMS** were created and controlled by a man who was a prisoner of his own destiny.

Later, after the storm had passed, everyone got to their feet and began looking over the ship for any possible damage. This time the air was warm and humid. It was daytime again. There were light scattered clouds above and they were now over water, but where? Their altitude was 2000 feet, and a lone sailing vessel below was sighted. Cobb got a better look through his telescope. He could see it was a Chinese junk.

"We're not over Russia anymore. I wonder what year this is," Cobb asked, handing the telescope to Raleigh.

"Well, either way there isn't much we can do about it. If Lionheart made no mention of our safe return, I would wonder if we would ever return to our home in our own time," she said.

They were traveling in a gentle wind, due west. After three hours, another ship was spotted. It too was a Chinese junk. An hour later, land came into view. Up ahead was the mouth of a river. There was a small fishing village at the river's edge. As they got closer, the buildings were unmistakable. Raleigh was right, they were off the coast of China somewhere. As they passed over the village, the people below waved.

"Well at least here the people are friendly," Cobb said, as he and the others waved back.

"This looks like it might be as good a place as any. We need to find level ground as soon as we can, to land the ship safely," Raleigh said.

"Agreed!" Cobb responded.

"Look!" Hadley yelled. Down the river ahead of them the blue lightning tunnel cloud of another time storm appeared. It was coming toward them. Raleigh tried to steer the ship away, but it was no use. The wind, blowing much stronger now, was pushing the ship directly into the cloud ahead.

"Everyone, brace yourselves!" Cobb yelled out as they were about to enter. Before them a horrifying sight unfolded. A giant dragon creature flew out of the cloud. "Christ-All-Mighty!" Cobb said, consumed in terror.

The beast circled the ship. As the Minerva entered the lightning cloud the creature turned away, flew past the village, and dove into the sea. Cobb could see it was trying to get out of the cloud storm. He was grateful for that. There were several moments of more terror as the lightning and thunder once again engulfed the ship.

101. AS THEY WERE ABOUT TO ENTER THE STORM, a horrifying sight unfolded. A giant dragon creature flew out of the cloud! "Christ-All-Mighty!" Cobb said, consumed in terror. After the beast circled the ship, it flew off toward the sea.

1554, Caribbean Sea

Later, after passing through another time storm, both Cobb and Raleigh were surprised to find the ship was somehow still flying. It was now early morning and calm. The sky was once again peaceful. Hermes came up next to the helm.

"It's over. The storms are through with us, or I should say Minerva," Hermes said, as he corrected himself.

Later, Cobb was able to rest in his cabin, but he wondered how long it had been since Raleigh or any of his crew rested. For an instant, he wondered if Raleigh needed rest. There was an island in the distance. The crew was looking over the latest damage. The storm claimed three more lives, McMillan, Marston, and Price. There was no trace of them. Cobb wondered about all the lives lost and what was yet to come.

"Captain, we're losing gas again. We lost the top replacement balloon. This time we can't stop the leaks!" Hadley reported.

The crew of the Minerva managed to land the ship safely on the island's north coast. They had landed on the Isla de Guanaja off the coast of Honduras. With just enough hydrogen remaining, the ship skidded up onto the beach before it came to rest. Everyone was exhausted. After resting, they looked over what was left of the ship and came to the quick conclusion that it would never fly again.

"Well, that's it for that!" Cobb said after a long pause. "How are we ever going to get off of this island?" he asked.

"Look!" Raleigh said, pointing at an approaching ship out in the horizon.

A day later, Cobb, Raleigh, and the rest of the crew were rescued by the Cargennia, a British cargo ship that was bound for America. A month later, Cobb was back in Waco, Texas. After the voyage, he maintained a good friendship with Raleigh. During the last storm, Captain Cobb's journal was lost. In the interest of not being labeled as a crazy person, he, Raleigh, and several surviving crew decided to make no mention of what happened after the giant octopus encounter. However, the story with Hermes illustrations later surfaced in a children's book written by his mother. It was the book that influenced Lionheart's design for the Onyx Tower.

1627, Proxima b

Captain's Log: We are now one month and eight days into our voyage which means back on Earth the date is August third, 1627. Having rode the space wave, we have returned to Proxima Centauri in the Alpha Centauri star system. With an orbit of 13,000 AU and an orbital period of a half million years, the Proxima Centauri star is distant from the other stars of Alpha Centauri. Proxima b will be our first interstellar port of call. We should be arriving there approximately 24 hours from now.

I confess my main interest in the Alpha Centauri system was the further exploration of the water world, Dark Neptune. That was the reason for making the Onyx Tower fully submersible. After surviving my first visit, I wanted to take a closer look at the aggressive lifeforms there. I didn't have the opportunity to properly catalog them after one of them nearly tore the Elisabeth starship apart.

I'm not sure why Ms. West was so insistent about Proxima b. I think West knows something about the calling card I discovered there on my first visit. At best Proxima b could be thought of as a strange, Earth like world that circles its star 22 times closer than Earth does the Sun. Even though it has three moons, the planet is tidally locked, always facing the Proxima star. Constant solar radiation striking the planet's light side has made the surface barren and hot, while the dark side is a constant frozen waste land. The only area tolerable is on the terminator. That is where the Totem Valley is located in the planet's northern hemisphere. I admit there is a strong possibility of life on both the light and dark sides of the planet, but for now my main interest is the world of Dark Neptune.

Peter M Lionheart, Captain

102. PROXIMA B LOOMS IN THE SKY above the Onyx Tower as it approaches the planet.

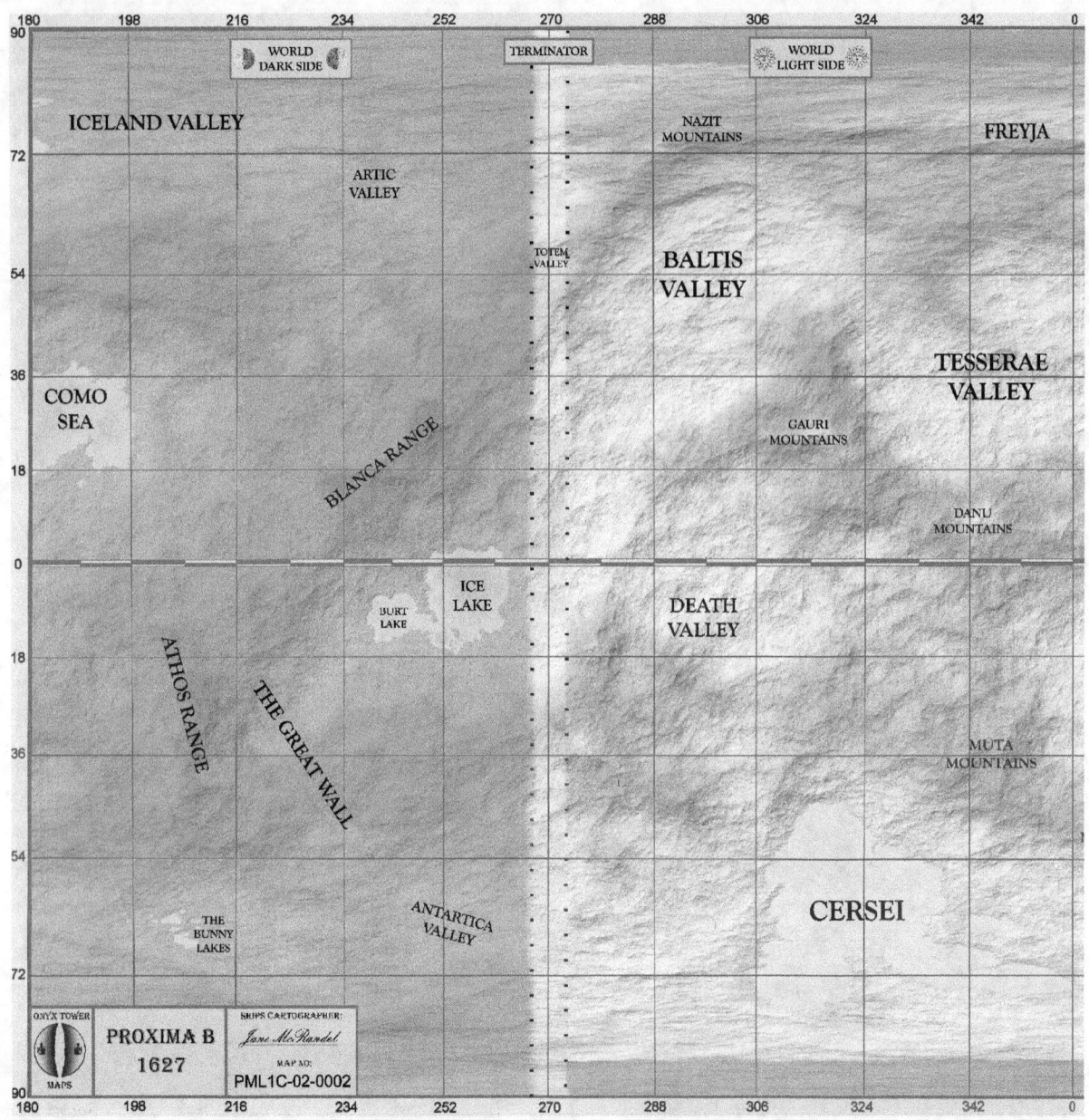

103. **THE WORLD OF PROXIMA B** as remastered by the ship's cartographer, Jane McRandel. Even though Lionheart had the world previously mapped from the Elisabeth's voyage, he wanted all previous destinations remastered for a master atlas he planned to create from the tower's voyages.

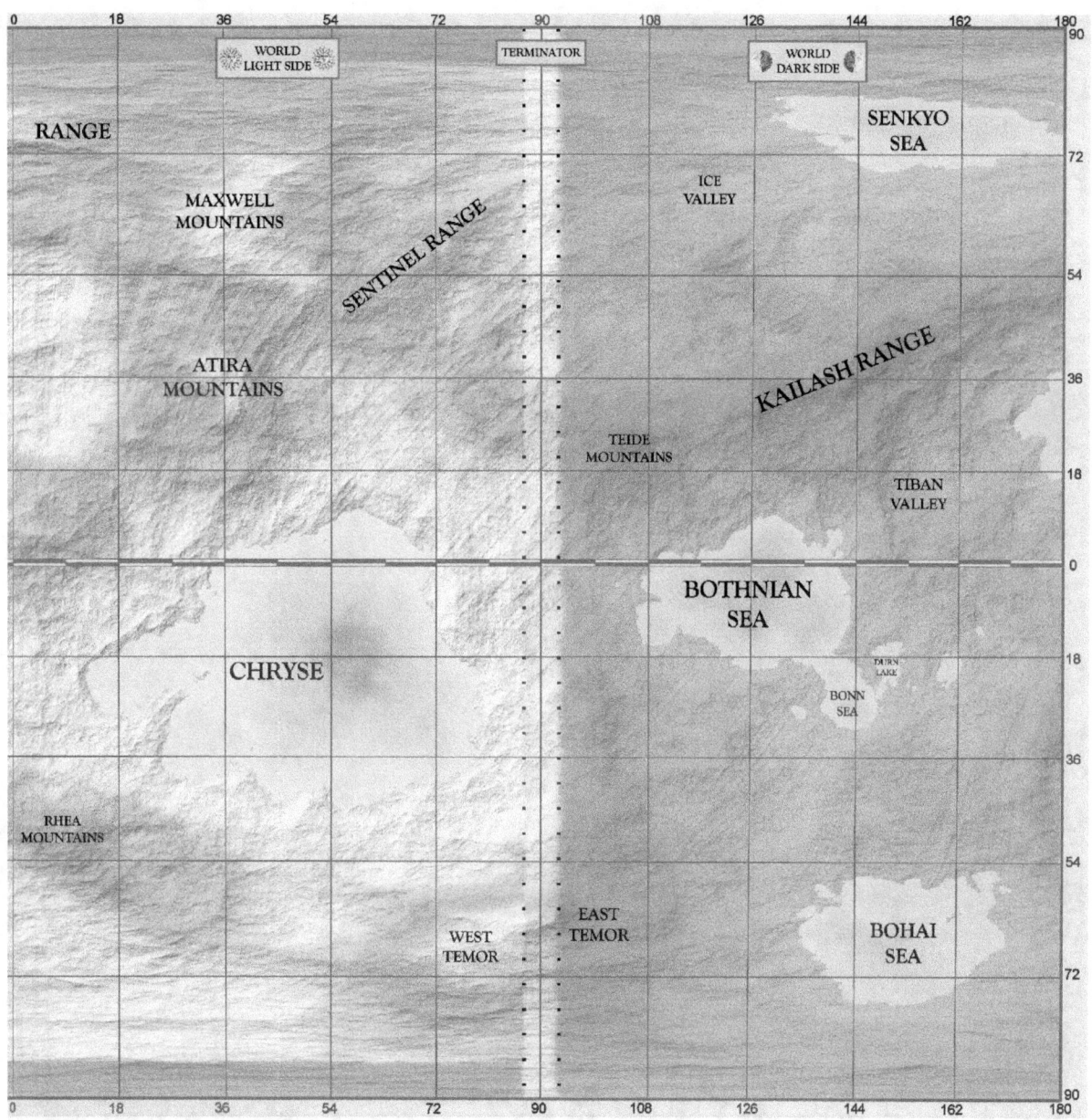

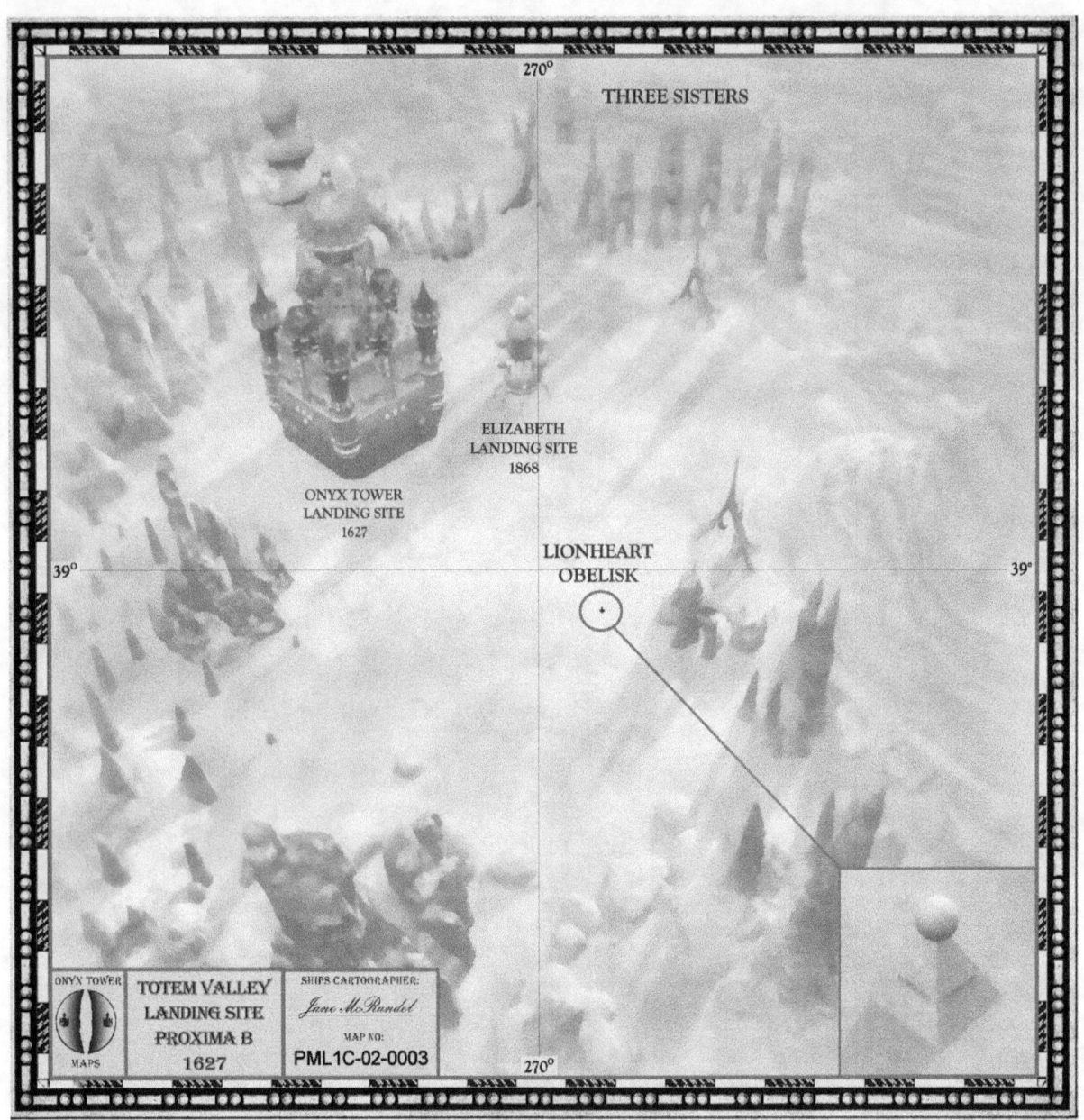

104. EVEN THOUGH THE TOWER had not yet landed, ship's cartographer, McRandel rendered the Totem Valley's landing site. She knew the tower would land to the west of the Elizabeth site so Lionheart could see the area where his previous ship will land in the future. Unknown to most, in his previous log, Lionheart recorded a large square depression in the ground to the west of the Elisabeth's landing site.

The Onyx Tower landed in the Totem Valley in the exact place where Lionheart noted the depression near the Elizabeth's landing site. Lionheart met with the landing party down in the launch bay. He saw that Ms. West had her creation loaded onto a forklift and had it covered. When he asked her about it, he only got the same answer *"you will understand"*. For a brief moment he thought of ordering her to answer, but because of his relationship with West, he decided to play along. As they made their way to the sight where he first came across the obelisk, he was surprised to see it wasn't there. He also noticed how barren the landscape was. When he arrived here the first time, there were patches of green moss everywhere. Upon arriving, Ms. West came alongside Lionheart and asked him where the exact spot of the obelisk had been. He pointed to an open area just ahead. West looked back at Elston and nodded her head. Elston and three others brought the forklift over and unloaded the covered object in the spot Lionheart had pointed to. With another nod, they unveiled the object. It was the obelisk. The exact same obelisk Lionheart saw on his first visit.

Not saying a word, Lionheart slowly walked over to it and touched its edge with the gloved hand of his suit. "This is it exactly. How did you know?" he asked quietly.

"Even though you were very careful not to reveal what you encountered here, I was able to find out. When I did, I became understandably curious of how it could have come about. I therefore began to run scenarios of possible events that could lead to the end result of such an encounter. After long careful thought, I was unable to reach a possible conclusion; that is, until our first encounter with the time storm."

105. **ONCE AGAIN IN THE TOTEM VALLEY,** Lionheart looks at the calling card that will inspire another, younger Lionheart when he arrives two and a half centuries from now.

"Then it all became very clear to me," West said as she continued. "When I observed that you were not taking any action, I deduced you had not reached the same conclusion that I came to. Knowing this I decided I had sufficient knowledge to create the calling card myself," West said.

"Calling card? I don't understand," Lionheart said.

"After reading of your experience here, I read of how it influenced you to undertake another interstellar journey and deplete every resource of your empire to create the Onyx Tower, a ship like no other. Had it not been for what you encountered here, none of it would have happened. Your life is on a path Captain, one which you must follow. It is one which will have an influence on all of humanity. Some parts of it are known to me. The calling card is only one piece of it," West explained.

Somewhat overwhelmed by what West said, Lionheart just stood silently for a moment with his hand still on the obelisk. "So, this was a calling card that was left for me. I understand. It all makes sense now. When I came here the first time, there was green moss growing everywhere," Lionheart said.

"Yes, it was life we accidently brought here from Earth. Much of this obelisk is made from soil taken from the lakebed we were on. When I read of your account of seeing moss here the first time you arrived, I deduced that it came from Earth and had taken root. It came from the soil used in making the obelisk," West said.

"So, we brought life here from Earth?"

"Yes, it will be no different than it was when sailing ships carried people to different parts of the Earth, so it will be with planets," West said.

"You said other parts of my life are known to you," Lionheart said.

"Yes," West answered.

"I don't suppose you can tell me anything."

"No."

"I know, in time I will understand," Lionheart said.

"Yes," West said.

After looking at the obelisk again, they headed back to the ship. As they got further away, Lionheart took one last look back at the obelisk, the calling card his younger self will encounter in the future. At that moment an unusual feeling came over him. He had the strong sensation that his new life was on a strange and wonderful course. He wondered about the adventures that awaited him and his crew, and yet he also felt a sense of rest and peace.

The End

The **Illustrated Tales From An Alternate Steampunk History** series is based on a collection of stories that were posted online over a period of several years. These stories cover the lives of characters, both good and evil, human, and non-human, natural or created, and some that live between the centuries. Throughout the timeline their lives and actions set off a chain reaction of events that create an extraordinary woven pattern of history that spans from the time of ancient periods to the centuries that lay ahead. The series is not limited to Earth or Human history, but also covers non-human, off-world events, some of which had an influence on humanity. Because of my interest in Steampunk, several stories take place in the 19th century where: genetic engineering, terraforming, and faster than light drive have become a reality with unexpected treasures and consequences.

ALSO AVAILABLE:

Tim Dooley's interest in 19th century science fiction goes back to the late 1950's after seeing the movie "The Fabulous World of Jules Verne". During the 70's and 80's, He illustrated fantasy machines that included airships, land steamers, flying machines, submarine steamships, off-world cities, planetary and interstellar spacecraft. In 1986 these drawings created an opportunity for him to work as a designer in the aerospace industry. In 1994, his drawings caught the attention of the woman who later became his wife. In 1997, one of the airship drawings he did was published in the Orange County Register's Focus on Science page. In 2003, he started creating scratch-built models of my own design for what he called "The Jules Verne Room". Over the years he posted illustrated stories all of which were based on an alternate steampunk timeline and is now in the process of converting them into a series of books.